W9-BTR-542

THE VANISHING ACT

THE VANISHING ACT

METTE JAKOBSEN

W. W. Norton & Company
New York · London

For Matilde

First American Edition 2012

Printed in the United States of America

For information about permission to reproduce selections from this book,
write to Permissions, W. W. Norton & Company, Inc.,
500 Fifth Avenue, New York, NY 10110

For information about special discounts for bulk purchases,
please contact W. W. Norton Special Sales at
specialsales@wwnorton.com or 800-233-4830

Manufacturing by Courier Westford
Book design by Susan Miller
Production manager: Devon Zahn

Library of Congress Cataloging-in-Publication Data

Jakobsen, Mette, 1964-
The vanishing act / Mette Jakobsen. — 1st American ed.
p. cm.
ISBN 978-0-393-06292-2 (hardcover)
I. Title.
PR9619.4.J35V36 2012
823'.92—dc23
2012021644

W. W. Norton & Company, Inc.
500 Fifth Avenue, New York, N.Y. 10110
www.wwnorton.com

W. W. Norton & Company Ltd.
Castle House, 75/76 Wells Street, London W1T 3QT

1 2 3 4 5 6 7 8 9 0

And the longer and more carefully
I examine all these things, the more
clearly and distinctly I know that
they are true.

René Descartes

It was snowing the morning I found the dead boy. The island with its two houses and one church was covered in a layer of white.

Papa was pulling in the fishing nets when I saw a hand between two rocks. It looked like a magic trick; almost as if a bunch of roses was about to appear—boom! *There you are, for you*—and then applause. But everything was quiet and the hand didn't move.

He was lying on his back, dusted with new snow in a cradle of rocks. His eyes were closed. A raven sat above him, watching from a weathered pine branch. The boy was a bit older than me, maybe fourteen or fifteen. His hair was dark, almost as dark as mine.

'Papa,' my voice came out as a whisper.

The dead boy's mouth was slightly open, as though he was about to ask a question, something hard to ask, something that made him hesitate.

'Papa,' I shouted, 'Papa.'

And then I started running towards him, stumbling, running, and Papa let the nets fall and caught me in his arms.

'Don't be scared, Papa,' I said against his thick coat, 'it's not Mama.'

Papa went to see the dead boy, and I waited at the fishing spot, watching how the wind picked up the fine snow and whirled it across rocks and sand. Winter had come early.

It was November. It had been a year since the circus. And a year since Mama walked out into the cold morning rain with a large black umbrella. A year since she disappeared, and took Turtle with her.

You might not believe my story. You might read it as a fairytale, a fable straight out of my imagination. But all of it is true. The dead boy stayed with us for three days. Papa laid him, frozen and stiff, on a bed in the blue room and that's where he remained until the delivery boat came. The island is still out there in the ocean; an island so tiny that it can't be found on any maps. Only a cross tells the weary sailor about the possibility of salvation in the middle of an endless sea.

Papa fished at dawn. His tin bucket sat in the cupboard under the sink and the nets hung on the back wall of the kitchen, where they looked dark and full of promise. Before Mama disappeared he would place her cup on the kitchen table and put water on the stove before he got the nets ready. Mama liked her coffee as soon as she got up. She liked it with cream and sugar in a delicate cup with small peacocks painted on the side. She would drink it slowly, with tousled hair and sleepy eyes.

I still got her cup out every morning and put it on the table. Papa would look sorrowfully at the fine porcelain. 'She is not dead, Papa,' I would tell him. 'She is coming back.'

I was twelve, my body thin and long, and I looked nothing like Mama. She was beautiful in a way I can't quite explain. But I can tell you that her eyes were grey, and even in the morning she wore dresses, blue, red or purple, and after her coffee she would put up her long red hair in a loose bun, in which she placed feathers or velvet roses.

The morning I found the dead boy, I gathered the nets while Papa finished his coffee, put on his boots and jacket and the yellow scarf I had knitted him the year before and that I could now see was less than perfect.

It was cold and dark outside, with only the lights from the church in the distance to guide us. Tiny, prickly snowflakes hit me hard on the cheeks and I shielded my eyes. We stood just outside the door, Papa and I. We couldn't see the ocean but we could hear it. The beach was two hundred and seventy-six steps from our front door. All that stood between the door and the beach was a pair of gigantic wrought-iron gates, which prevailed tall and proud. They were wishing, I imagined, for the fence that had never followed. Theodora, who built the church and the two houses on the island more than two hundred years earlier, died an untimely death and never got around to making the fence.

'Are you ready?' Papa put the nets over his shoulder.

'I can't find my gloves.'

'Have mine.'

He handed me his large gloves with sheep's wool lining, and reached for his bucket, while the fading night rushed towards us, as if it had just one last chance to make itself felt.

Papa always opened the gates instead of walking around them. 'A gentleman never ignores a gate,' he declared. The gates swung closed behind us with a rusty shriek, and Papa said, as he always did, 'Name me three philosophers, Minou.'

And that morning, as on every other morning, I had three names ready for him. 'Kant, Hegel and Descartes, of course.'

'Of course,' he said and took my hand. I couldn't see his face, but I knew he was pleased, and together we stepped down the path, and then along the beach, like two blind explorers, through seaweed and dark rocks, through ice and sea moss, towards the fishing spot.

Papa said that to live on an island was to live in a closed fist. 'Nothing suits a philosopher better,' he said. 'How can you philosophise if you constantly have to choose?' On an island as small as ours there were choices to be made, but not that many. Most of the time could be spent thinking, which for Papa was the noblest of all pursuits.

I could walk around the island in fifty-three minutes. It was the shape of the chocolate cat-tongues we sometimes had for Christmas. They were creamy and milky with a shape more like a dog's bone than a cat's tongue. At the western point was Theodora's Plateau. I was never allowed to go close to the edge. The wind alone, said Papa, could whisk you off and fling you into the waves far below.

Had the boy arrived on the island alive and well, we would have shown our visitor around. We would walk from the beach and up the path. And Papa would tell the boy everything about the old lighthouse that sat on top of our house and leaned slightly towards the sea. It was no longer in use. But Papa was proud of it, and, even though he wasn't very practical, he had spent many hours repairing the outside wooden stairs to the lighthouse so it could be my special place.

As we got closer I would say to the boy, 'Just wait until you get inside the house, just wait until you see the walls.' Because Mama liked to paint and had filled the house with colourful murals.

And I would whisper to the boy that everyone thought that Mama was dead. Priest had found her shoe washed up on the beach after she disappeared. Papa never spoke of the day they put it, salt-stained and minus its heel, in an old shoebox and buried it. I watched the funeral from the lighthouse. Papa had wanted me to go, but I said no. I said that it was of no use: I was sure that Mama was still alive.

We would show the boy the forest with its seventeen pines, its many rabbits and the old apple tree that one summer bore three hundred and two apples. We would lead him along the forest path and visit Boxman and his faithful companion, No Name, a short dog, with scruffy white fur and floppy ears.

Then we would go to visit Priest. And the church would look magnificent in the morning darkness, with light spilling from every window and scores of ravens flying in and out of the bell tower.

'Priest is scared of the dark,' I would explain. 'He sleeps in the tower and keeps the light on all night. That's why we don't need a new lighthouse. Sometimes when he is upset he even rings the bell.'

Later I would show the boy the rusty machine that sat in a shed next to the church, wheezing and coughing, making light for the whole island.

'Not all islands have light,' I would explain.

And the boy would be impressed that we had both light, and a church complete with Priest and bell tower on an island so small.

In the centre of the lighthouse was an enormous bulb. Once I tried to switch it on, but Papa got angry.

'There is mercury in it,' he said and rubbed his nose where his reading glasses had left a red mark. 'It's poisonous. That's why so many lighthouse keepers have gone mad living here. They saw things rising out of the sea: strange creatures, pirate ships, goats, pigs, all sorts of scary things.'

'And horses, Papa?'

'Anything that shouldn't come out of the water in the first place.'

On the big bulb I stuck the four pictures of Descartes that Uncle had given to me. He came to visit when Mama disappeared. Uncle was Papa's brother, and he was the one who had traced our family line right back to Descartes. He was an academic and worked in the Department of Paranormal Sciences at a renowned university. Uncle was the only one left in the department and worked from an office so small that he had to leave his briefcase outside the door.

I had spent every night in the lighthouse since Mama disappeared. I had an old mattress with lots of blankets, and a small heater in the corner. But Papa still tucked me into bed downstairs each evening and made sure that I was wearing a scarf, jacket and a thick jumper before I got under the covers. Then he kissed me goodnight, checked that my boots were ready next to the bed and turned the lights out.

Sometimes I stayed in bed for a while, listening to Papa in the study, to his absent humming and the sound of pages being turned, but most nights I would get up, tiptoe down the hallway, quietly open the front door and climb the outside staircase to the lighthouse.

The ceiling in the lighthouse was low and I could only just stand up in the middle. I would sit, wrapped in blankets, looking out at the island: a dark shape of sand, snow and rocks, searching my mind for something surprising that I could tell Mama when she came back.

I once asked Papa what philosophers think about. We were in the kitchen. Mama was on her knees, paint on her cheek, putting the final touches on a picture of the old apple tree.

'They think about life,' he said.

'About dogs?' I asked.

'No, they don't worry too much about dogs.'

'About trees then?'

'No, not about trees either, they don't think in specifics, they think broadly.'

'About the island?'

'No,' said Papa, 'they think about much bigger things.'

'The stars?'

'Not necessarily. Philosophers step back and look at the big picture.'

'That is not what Mama does.'

'No,' Papa agreed.

'She says the tiniest brush stroke matters.'

'But sometimes, my girl, when you look in such detail, you lose the big picture.'

'What is the big picture, Papa?'

'Truth, the absolute truth, Minou. Telling us why things happen.'

'What things?'

'Things that are not easy to understand.'

'Things about the war, Papa?'

'Yes, Minou. Most definitely things about the war.'

'But what if someone doesn't want to see the big picture?' I asked.

'Well,' Papa hesitated, 'that would be a pity, Minou.' He glanced at Mama. Her painting, he said, would be a great addition to the kitchen. The tree's wilted branches stretched around the front door and touched the umbrella stand. And beside the rack where her shoes were lined up in neat rows she had painted a rabbit with extra long ears and next to it a pile of delicious-looking apples.

Mama didn't care much for philosophy. 'Use your imagination Minou,' she would say, 'don't think so much.'

Once she took the leaf I had carefully pressed in Papa's copy of Kant's *Critique of Pure Reason* and held it up to the window. The leaf was dry and brittle and little squares of light shone through it.

'What does it look like?' She held it higher for me to see.

I shook my head.

'Make something up, Minou. Something curious.'

I hesitated, looking hard at the leaf.

'Can't you see the city and all the houses? And there—' she pointed, 'a square, where everyone gathers at night.'

'Who?' I asked.

'All the people in the city, of course,' she laughed, then looked at me. 'Where is your imagination, Minou? Where has it gone?'

After Mama disappeared I asked Papa to order a notebook from the boatmen. It had two hundred and ten pages. And in it I wrote down everything that happened, such as:

> There is one apple left on the tree, Mama.
>
> It's very cold. Papa says that winter has come early. If you are on a boat I hope you can keep warm.
>
> Last night I forgot to shut the front door properly. Papa's glass of water turned to ice overnight.
>
> Yesterday Papa caught nineteen fish, a record!
>
> There is snow on your shoe-grave.

And I drew the pinecones I kept in the lighthouse. I documented their shape and height and each day I would add more raven bones to my collection, trying to arrange them into different patterns, hoping to see something special that Mama might like. But I felt silly, remembering Papa's words. 'A philosopher sees with his rational mind, Minou, he does not engage with the imagination. It takes us to unpredictable places, it follows our wishes and wants, not what really is.' I thought it might help if I knew more about where Mama had come from and what she did before she arrived on the island. But she never talked about her past—not to me, not to Papa. She told Papa that she had been in the war, but would not tell him what had happened to her. All Papa really knew was that she had arrived on the island in a rowboat on a windy day, with a red suitcase and her pet peacock called Peacock.

Papa and Priest lived on the island when Mama came, Boxman came later still. Priest had been there the longest, and said that nothing was better for a man of God than to be in a quiet place. The only time he had tried to go back was when the war broke out. He wanted to help, but no delivery boat would take him.

Papa arrived after the war and liked the quiet life on the island straight away. He enjoyed the occasional meal with priest and was content without a wife.

Mama wasn't looking to get married either, she said. She just needed a hot cup of coffee and a place to put down her suitcase. But when she saw Papa waving from the shore, she liked him straight away.

'Imagine, little one. A kind and gentle man waving to me, almost as if he had been waiting for me to arrive.'

Papa remembered the day clearly, every little bit of it, he said. It was cold and the sky was grey. Ravens flew out to sea the way they always did when a boat approached, but were thrown back, one after the other, Mama said, like funny old hats, twirling, tumbling towards shore.

'She was a most unexpected sight,' said Papa. 'So colourful.'

Mama's red hair had shone and glinted in the bleak sunlight, and when the rowboat got closer Papa spotted Peacock sitting contentedly in a golden bowl, showing off his brilliantly blue tail feathers.

Papa gallantly helped her out of the boat and invited her in for a cup of coffee. He knew that she had come a long way when he saw the autumn leaves in her hair. They were not from an apple tree. He was certain of that. And, while Mama drank her coffee, Papa got out an old bone-comb from an otherwise empty drawer. Then slowly and patiently, as though sorting through his fishing nets, he combed her hair.

Mama had painted her arrival, filling an entire wall in the blue room. Her painting showed a life-size rowboat with a ruffled Peacock staring confidently into the giant waves. Mama had painted herself waving and smiling, and she had painted Papa on the shore. He looked kind as he waved back, shielding his eyes from the sun.

'I knew he was a good man as soon as he took my hand and helped me ashore,' Mama would say and look at Papa affectionately.

Papa always said that the war was still inside him. Sometimes I thought I could feel it when I held his hand. He had spent the entire war hiding amongst onions and carrots in a small root cellar the size of a cupboard. But when I wanted to hear more about the cellar Papa would say, 'You are far too young, my girl. Later.'

I asked Mama if she had felt the war in Papa's hand when he had reached out and helped her safely to the shore.

'Yes, little one,' she answered and looked out towards the sea. 'It runs in me as well.'

It was a slow walk from the beach to our house. Papa carried the dead boy. He was frozen and very heavy. One of his hands reached stiffly in front of him as though he was blind and not quite trusting Papa's steps. I had never seen a dead person before, only the ravens and rabbits I sometimes found on the island. And Peacock, of course, when he died of old age. But the dead boy was different.

Priest was doing his Japanese morning exercises in the distance. I could see him in front of the church, stretching backwards, crying out as he always did, sounding, Papa said, like a deer on heat.

'You have to pretend you are a warrior,' Priest explained.

I thought he said 'worrier' and believed he was doing an excellent job until Papa corrected me.

When Papa later told Mama, she laughed so hard she almost cried.

As I watched the dead boy's lifeless face move stiffly against Papa's shoulder, I remembered how Mama looked that day. Her face had been flushed and warm from laughing.

'Oh dear,' she had said when I got annoyed. Then she hugged me. 'It's just funny little one. Don't worry.' And with that she started again, a low deep chuckle.

Just before the gates the dead boy lost his shoe. I picked it up. It was large, brown and waterlogged. Papa had insisted that the dead boy was going to stay at our house and not on the beach. And, shoe in hand, I reluctantly opened the gates for them.

We never used the blue room. It was Mama's and had been hers, said Papa, from the moment she arrived on the island. It had a narrow cast-iron bed, and a rickety table crowded with paintbrushes, piles of paper and an old cookie tin filled with the flowers and feathers she used for her hair. Next to the table sat her red suitcase.

'There is nothing to worry about, my girl,'

Papa puffed as he manoeuvred the boy onto the squeaking bed.

'How long is he going to stay?' I demanded from the doorway.

'Until the delivery boat comes. Three days.' Papa stood back from the bed and exhaled.

The dead boy was lying on his back. His leg was bent as though he was a dancer caught in an impossible jump. His bare foot was the colour of raven bones, his toenails black.

'Don't let the heat get in, Minou. He needs to stay frozen.' Papa opened the window wide, then checked the temperature on the old thermometer nailed next to Mama's mural. 'It's already two degrees celsius,' he stated. 'That's excellent. If we keep the window open it will turn into a freezer in here.'

'Why is his mouth like that?' I stepped inside and closed the door behind me.

'He might have died saying something, Minou.'

'What, Papa?'

'He could have been talking to someone. But there is no way of knowing what he said.'

'Where does he come from?'

'I am not sure, my girl. I must say, this is a rare occurrence. Most unusual.'

And while Papa attempted to put a pillow under the dead boy's head, I realised that this was it. This was the special thing I had been searching for. There was so much we could tell Mama about the dead boy. She would want to hear everything. And she would no longer mind that Papa liked philosophy or that the water pipes froze during winter.

When the pipes froze Papa would get his tools and lay them out on the kitchen bench. Mama would look at him.

'Don't worry,' he once assured her, 'I know how to fix them. It all comes down to logic.'

'Logic?' Mama replied.

'I can fix them,' Papa repeated, looking worried. 'It's only ice.'

'It's this house,' said Mama, her voice rising like a wave, 'this island, don't you see?' And then she went out without a coat on and was gone for hours.

Mama always walked around the island when she was upset. I would see her from the lighthouse, throwing rocks into the sea at Theodora's Plateau, looking as if she walked a tightrope between earth and sky.

But the dead boy would change all that.

'How did he look?' she would ask, and then,

without waiting for an answer, she would turn to Papa and say, 'And you carried him all that way!'

Papa would nod modestly and Mama would be impressed. Then she would say again and again, 'Oh, I wish I had been there. Tell me everything, absolutely everything.'

Snowflakes whirled through the window like uninvited guests, and Papa was right, the room turned cold almost in an instant.

'You can put his shoe next to the bed, Minou.'

I stepped closer and placed the shoe on the floor and put my hand in Papa's.

'He smells of oranges,' I said.

Papa nodded. 'Yes, even though he is frozen. It's extraordinary. He almost smells like the orange cake your Mama used to bake. Did I ever tell you,' he continued, not for the first time, 'that I found twenty-seven leaves in her hair the day she arrived? In the most magnificent autumn colours. And I put them on the table, one next to the other according to size.' Papa paused. 'Your mama, she looked at me with a smile, took my hand and said, as if it wasn't a question at all, "Would you like to marry me?" But I knew, even before she reached the shore, that she was for me. So you see, Minou, all I had to do was to say, "Yes."'

We left the dead boy in the blue room and spent the rest of that day in Papa's study. Papa worked every day. Ever since the war he had tried to find the absolute truth, the one from which everything can be explained and understood.

Theodora, the first to settle on the island, had been a philosopher too. Her diary, kept next to the altar in the church, was full of philosophical notes, most of them on Aristotle, whom she greatly admired. Without his reasoning, she said, not a single house would have been built on the island. One of Theodora's great mottos was 'Reason conquers all.' And it encouraged Papa to think that Theodora had been sitting in the same study more than two hundred years earlier, searching for the truth just like him.

There were many things to look at in Papa's study, but the thing you noticed was the wall filled with postcards from Grandfather.

Grandfather had already found the absolute truth, but wanted Papa to find it on his own. Truth is not worth having, and can never be fully understood, said Grandfather, unless you find it yourself. But he did try to help Papa. The last few years of his life, before he was hit by lightning and died, he sent weekly clues to Papa by postcard.

All the postcards featured a picture of the same mechanical horse. It was the invention of a seventeenth-century alchemist and was created for warfare. The horse looked mean, but Papa said it was a flight of the imagination and that the invention had never worked.

'That horse never trotted anywhere,' he would say.

I asked Papa if Grandfather liked horses, but Papa didn't think so. He said that Grandfather didn't like spending money on anything, and that it was more likely that he had got a good deal buying the postcards in bulk.

Mama would read each clue aloud with a sigh: 'Particular existence.' 'The organ of happiness.' 'Twofold and then more.' 'Finite and boundless consciousness.'

Sometimes Papa got worried about the public display of Grandfather's truth, but comforted himself with the thought that the boatmen who ran the delivery boat weren't philosophers and probably wouldn't know what to do with these fragments. He stuck the postcards up in his study, one next to the other, until they filled the entire wall, and by the time Grandfather died there were two hundred and twelve cards all attached with drawing pins. Sometimes Papa would shuffle them around and study them again.

The day I found the dead boy I sat on the floor in Papa's study and wrote in my notebook, while he worked at his desk. I wrote:

> I found a dead boy, Mama.
>
> He is in the blue room on your bed. We opened the window. Papa says that he needs to stay frozen.
>
> He will be with us for three days until the delivery boat comes.
>
> I will draw him for you tomorrow when Papa goes fishing.
>
> I wish you would come home, Mama.

I also added that the dead boy's eyes might be

brown like mine, but that I couldn't be sure because they were closed. Then I drew the raven that I remembered sitting on the broken pine branch over the dead boy, snow resting on its feathers like a white coat. I also drew Papa's tin bucket, abandoned, full of fish on the beach, and described how their tails made a sad song against the side of the bucket as we walked away.

Once in a while Papa stretched, put down his pen and said, 'Let's go and see the dead boy, Minou.' And together we crossed the corridor and opened the door to the blue room. On our first visit Papa went straight to the window and opened it wider.

'Don't be afraid, Minou,' he said, when he saw me lingering near the door.

Then he walked over to the bed, reached out and felt the dead boy's hand. 'Death is a natural part of life. We all end up like this. It's perfectly logical.'

I walked a bit closer. Then I did what Papa had done. I reached out and touched the dead boy's hand. His skin was hard, but soft and wet at the same time. It almost felt like No Name's nose on an icy day.

'See,' Papa looked at me approvingly. 'Nothing to be scared of.'

By evening Papa seemed unusually happy.

He was writing at the desk with amazing speed, muttering 'arrival,' 'dead,' 'coincidence,' and 'oranges,' as I picked out coloured pencils from a drawer, planning to draw the dead boy at first light.

Papa stopped writing, his pen poised above the paper. 'This is what your grandfather used to talk about,' he said, looking at me, his reading glasses perched on his nose.

'What, Papa?' I asked.

'The great coincidences,' he said. 'They wake you up, Minou; they shake you like the wind shakes the apple tree. They point towards something you might have forgotten.'

'But what are the great coincidences, Papa?'

'Things that make you stop and think, Minou.' Papa jotted something down on his pad, then looked at me again. 'Your grandfather once came across a salmon when he was swimming in a river. It swam right up close, almost as if it wanted to tell him something. At that time your grandfather was working on a particularly difficult philosophical question and the salmon, Minou, reminded him of how fishing often remains good in one spot, even though the current constantly changes. I am still not sure exactly how, but I know that seeing that salmon changed everything for your grandfather. His philosophy was never the same again. He even painted a salmon above the door to his house.'

I must have looked uncertain, because Papa added in a convincing voice, 'This boy, Minou, is one of those great coincidences. He is reminding me of something. Something to do with the truth.' Papa took off his reading glasses and stroked the bridge of his nose. 'I might sit with him tonight, my girl. We haven't had anyone visiting for a long time, not since your uncle. It's nice to have company again, don't you think?'

I wasn't quite sure but I knew that Mama would be excited to hear about the dead boy when she came home. And the house was filled with delicious wafts of orange and it was true, it felt as if Mama was baking again.

Before I went to the lighthouse that night I opened the door to the blue room. In the darkness lay the dead boy and on the windowsill sat a raven, silent and black. I stood in the doorway feeling the cold, seeing my breath unfurl like a sea mist, and whispered, 'I will see you in the morning.'

I woke in the lighthouse in the middle of the night. Papa was speaking to the dead boy. His voice rose, muffled and deep, through the floorboards. I couldn't hear what he was saying, but he sounded happy. For a moment I even thought I heard him laugh. I lay awake listening to him, while snow whirled and pricked the lighthouse windows.

Papa didn't laugh very often. 'Life is not about feeling happy,' he would say. 'It is about being prepared.'

'Poor old man,' Mama would say. 'No truth could ever prepare you for the cellar.'

Papa would shake his head and say, 'It's not just about the cellar.'

'My dear.' Mama would look at him kindly. 'This—' she made a gesture towards the bookshelf and the open notebooks on his desk '—is all about the cellar.'

I kept listening to Papa's voice. Tiny snowflakes seemed to fall endlessly in the dark-blue of the night. I could see the outline of the forest with its apple tree and seventeen pines, and through the forest a small path, a grey winding rope leading to Boxman's yard. Light spilled out of Boxman's open door, and just outside sat his dog, No Name, a dark shadow with spindly legs and floppy ears.

I sat up, wrapped the blankets around me, and reached for the scarf I was knitting. It was orange. Boxman had admired it when I showed it to him. 'You are an expert knitter, Minou,' he said. Then he proceeded to tell me that the scarf was the exact same colour as a circus tent he once worked in.

Mama and I liked everything to do with the circus and we would visit Boxman every day. Mama said magic tricks were one of just a few good reasons to live.

Boxman had only been on the island a year

when Mama disappeared. He wore his hair in a ponytail and was younger than both Papa and Priest. Cosmina, a French actress, had left him, and he had come to the island to mend his broken heart.

Boxman used to work in a circus, but after arriving on the island he began to make boxes for magicians. The kind in which women are sawn in half.

'I believe in love,' he said, 'and there is nothing, absolutely nothing, more beautiful than a woman just rescued from a box.'

His boxes were beautiful, too; inlaid with satin, painted in bright colours with gold lettering.

Boxman never asked if I could see into his yard from the lighthouse, and I didn't think he knew that I sometimes watched him. One night he was teaching No Name how to jump through hoops of fire. The blue flames cast strange shadows on the barn, and I could smell the petrol.

No Name didn't like it. He did it once, burned himself, then refused to do it again. On Boxman's naked chest was a birthmark, large and purple, right where his heart was. He had a heart on the outside.

Another time, early in the morning when I could smell Papa's coffee and was about to go downstairs,

Boxman came out wearing his usual blue cape and a black top hat. He took off the hat in a smooth movement, paused theatrically, and then pulled out a rabbit. Its grey fur shone a brilliant silver in the morning light. I could see its dark eyes, its quivering nose, and I wondered how Boxman did it, and whether the smile he sent in my direction was intended for me.

After the episode with the hoops I made a scarf for No Name to cover the burnt patches, and reminded Boxman, who didn't always think of these things, that under no circumstances was No Name allowed to jump through fire with the scarf on.

Boxman's house was more like a barn. He had a cooker in the corner where he made tea and a foldout bed where he slept. And his piano accordion was always close by. One wall of Boxman's barn was stacked with wooden boxes, ready to be painted.

The barn smelled of hay and sawdust and the green jelly-like soap that he used to clean his hands after painting. On another wall hung photographs and 'thank you' notes from magicians all over the world. Most of them were waving and smiling next to their newly acquired boxes, but one magician looked serious. He stood in what appeared to be a snowstorm, next to a tiger in a cage, wearing a long brown coat, and an enormous black moustache that glinted against the white. The tiger looked at him with great interest and, I thought, something that looked like a hungry smile.

The autograph read:

The Great Shine
Magician and Illusionist
~
Before you know it you are gone!

Out of the thirty-three photographs on the wall, that was Mama's favourite. She often stood for a long time in front of The Great Shine.

'What a life,' she sighed. 'What an incredible life.' Then she would shake her head in wonderment, 'He looks like a man of the world.'

'He is,' said Boxman. 'A courageous one. He went from Moscow to Siberia on a rusty bike just to learn a new trick. He had to eat potatoes all the way, and lost his left foot to frostbite. Imagine the commitment.' Boxman looked at The Great Shine.

'He even found the tiger on the way and tamed it. An incredible man.'

I think most of Boxman's admiration came from the potato thing. He hated potatoes and said they tasted like sucking on a coin. But I didn't like the sound of tigers running wild. You would have to pedal very fast, just in case, and I didn't think it would be much fun to lose your foot either.

You couldn't see his feet in the photograph. He was standing knee-deep in snow. But when Mama later painted a life-size mural of The Great Shine and his tiger on our living room wall, she added a shiny metal boot to his left foot.

I knitted slowly and looked out into the night. Boxman had started to play the accordion and No Name was still sitting outside the barn door, his head turned towards the sky and the falling snow.

When the wind blew in the right direction we could hear Boxman play as clearly as if he was sitting in our living room. Boxman was good at a lot of things. He built magic boxes, made things vanish with a flash of his silk handkerchief, and he was good at juggling. He could throw balls high into the air—one, two, three, four, five—and one after the other they would move in a perfect arc between his hands, again, again. They went so fast that it was impossible to follow them. Boxman had tried to teach me, but said that I was thinking too much.

'When you are juggling,' he said, 'there is only room for your hands and the balls, nothing else. You have to put your mind elsewhere.'

'Where?' I asked.

'In a drawer, in a box, outside the door, it doesn't really matter, Minou, as long as you are able to find it again.'

Mama said circus tricks reminded her that the war was over and that she could breathe once again.

'Those monstrous people,' she said, doing a sketch of No Name as he sat on my lap. 'Make him sit still, Minou.'

'Why were they monstrous, Mama?'

'They didn't know about magic, little one. They didn't know what it means to have imagination.' Mama paused, looking at her drawing, pencil pressed against her lips. 'Even if they stood on the highest mountaintop, Minou, they still wouldn't be able to see it. They were like dogs.'

'Dogs?'

'He won't understand what I am saying, Minou. Take your hands off his ears.'

I hesitated, then uncovered No Name's ears.

'Dogs of war, Minou, because they were loyal to ideas and leaders without ever questioning them.' Mama added a final line to the drawing. 'They had forgotten to use their minds properly.'

'No Name is not like that,' I said, and pulled his solid, furry body a bit closer.

'No,' Mama smiled, 'he is indeed an entirely different kind of dog.'

The heater in the lighthouse hummed in the corner and Boxman had started a new tune. It was fast. It jumped and hopped like a runner over a rocky beach. I thought of the morning when I had just turned ten. The sun had risen, and I was running around the entire island. Papa had timed me, hunched over in the lighthouse with his big stopwatch waving every time we could see each other. It had taken me just twenty-eight minutes to run the whole island, and my feet had felt as if they were flying. Papa had said that I had looked like a strong gazelle in flight.

I stopped knitting and looked into Boxman's

yard again. No Name had gone back inside. He was probably curled up in the corner of the barn, sleeping against a bale of hay.

'What's the hay for?' I asked Boxman one day when the wind was howling and the snow falling thick. Mama and I were sitting next to Boxman on the apothecary's desk with its hundred and fifty-nine small drawers, each labelled in a delicate hand, with words like Screws, Magic Rope, Problems, Sugar.

We were sitting close together, keeping warm, reading some of Boxman's magazines. Two rabbits were nibbling with furious speed on one of Boxman's cabbages and we could see No Name through the open door, trying to catch snowflakes in the yard.

'I might get a goat one day,' he answered, 'like Theodora.'

Boxman was wearing heavy boots, his cape and the dark blue scarf I had knitted him. He looked like a prince.

'A goat would be fun, you could come and sing for it,' he said to Mama, who smiled.

'Do goats like music?' I asked.

'I am sure that they do,' he said. 'You could sing too.'

'I can't sing.'

'I think you can,' said Boxman.

'No,' I said. 'I can't.'

'You just have to pretend that you are the centre of the universe.'

Mama nodded and said, 'Like a bird in a tree, with the most splendid view.'

'Or like an elephant eating apples,' added Boxman. 'You can play Beethoven's fifth right next to them and they won't hear the slightest thing if there are apples on the menu.'

I shook my head, confused. 'But how can I pretend to be the centre of the universe?'

Then Boxman showed us a slim microscope that was a gift from Cosmina. She was Boxman's great love, and used to assist him in the box trick. Cosmina had curly hair, red like Mama's, and Boxman said that she was a wonderful actress. She would lie in the box, crying out for help so urgently that his heart ached as he sawed through the wood.

Cosmina, Boxman told us, used to jump out of the box and cling to his chest, 'Oh,' she would cry, 'Oh, I thought I was going to die. I truly thought I was going to die.'

But one day Cosmina no longer wanted to be rescued. Boxman suspected that it was because of their new trick. After they had added a vanishing act to their performance, Cosmina began to talk about things she had never mentioned before. During breaks and costume changes she spoke about stars, endlessness, and the rapture of the night, and she no longer seemed happy when he rescued her from the box. It wasn't long before she told Boxman she had found herself, and wanted to study the stars from the foothills of the Himalayas. She had read about Galileo and wanted to walk in his footsteps.

'Did Galileo go to the Himalayas?' I asked.

'I don't think so,' said Boxman, 'but he probably dreamt about it. It would be just like Cosmina to keep someone else's dream alive, she was such a kind soul.'

The day before she left, Cosmina gave Boxman the microscope.

'Observe,' she told him. 'What you see is the universe in a tiny drop. From this you will know yourself to be the centre from which everything unfolds, all colour, all movement, everything.'

Boxman unwrapped the microscope from layers of soft cloth and in the darkness of the barn I put my eye to the lens and saw tiny stars in a piece of hay, and in a scrap of newspaper I saw the Milky Way, looking exactly as it did on a particularly clear night. I felt dizzy from the sight, but it still didn't feel as if I was the centre of anything.

'Do you feel dizzy when you look at the stars?' I asked Boxman.

'No,' said Boxman, 'but I think No Name does.'

And it was true, on clear nights No Name would growl at the stars and at the same time look longingly towards them, in a way that made him seem a bit crazy.

I laughed as No Name continued his frantic pirouettes around the snowflakes. 'He doesn't know where he is going,' I said.

Looking at him I thought that maybe he could see the universe in the snow, and that perhaps it was all too much for him.

'No Name knows exactly what he is doing,' said Boxman. 'His steps are measured, so that he can experience the delicious feeling—'

'Of not making sense,' finished Mama. And they both laughed.

That didn't sound right. I liked logic and at that moment No Name looked more crazy with longing than as if he was feeling something delicious. He looked as though he had forgotten which way was home.

Later I thought that with a proper name No Name might have a better sense of direction and wouldn't wear himself out so much when it was snowing, and it was clear to me that neither Boxman nor Mama knew about logic the way Papa and I did.

I had tried to knit with gloves on, but it was difficult. The glass panes that made up the walls of the lighthouse were not thick enough to withstand the elements. And even though the heater was on throughout the night, the knitting needles were always cold. Every so often I put my hands under the blankets, and kept them pressed against my warm belly until I was ready to knit again.

Sometimes I wished that No Name would keep me company at night. He was always warm, no matter what. But he didn't like the lighthouse. The one time I carried him up the wooden stairs and put him next to the big bulb, he howled so loud that Priest could hear him from the back of the church. Priest had just turned on his noisy industrial oven, about to bake his weekly supply of pretzels, and said that it must have been a howl without precedent.

'No Name is not a dog that appreciates a good view,' said Boxman. 'Some dogs do, but we don't choose our personality, Minou.'

If No Name had liked the tower I could have talked to him about Mama and about philosophy, and all the things I thought about while knitting. I could have told him about the great coincidences and Grandfather's salmon. And how Papa, even though he didn't want to tell me about the root cellar, shared everything philosophical with me.

Papa had realised early on, he said, that I had a talent for philosophy. One of the first signs was that I liked going for walks in the morning all by myself.

'All philosophers walk,' Papa explained, 'Kierkegaard, Descartes, Kant, Nietzsche, all of them. They walk along empty beaches with cold hands and windblown faces, searching their minds for the truth.'

I liked the beach early in the morning. The horizon would appear suddenly, as if someone had decided, said Mama, to paint two bold strokes on the night sky. And the beach changed overnight. There was much to be found along the water's edge. Sometimes I forgot to think philosophical thoughts and stopped to collect raven bones and shiny shells among the rocks. If I were lucky I would find a whole raven skeleton. They were beautiful, with black beaks and bones the colour of sand. Their skulls were the size of Boxman's juggling balls, round and smooth with deep indentations where their eyes had been. Their necks looked like knots on a thick string of wool and their wings were still adorned with feathers. I had three of them in the tower in my collection of bones.

Papa never waved if we met on the beach on our solitary morning walks. He just stared into the sand and dark rocks and I tried to do the same. But if I happened to meet Mama I would stop and talk to her. She liked finding things, too, and had collected a rusty bike with bent wheels that Boxman unsuccessfully tried to fix for me, and half a violin with two strings that Mama thought looked like an unusual boat, in which you could go to unusual places.

Kant, Papa told me, took the same walk every day. He left his house at half past three every afternoon, timing his departure with such precision that neighbours, shopkeepers, the shoeshine man on the corner, and whoever else saw him adjusted their watches as he passed. He walked down the same streets, through the same park, passing the same shops and, just before turning the last corner into his street, he would admire the same large chestnut tree.

But one day the chestnut was gone. In its place were blue sky and a straight view to Madam Trapp's laundry. On the footpath sat neat stacks of firewood. Kant went to bed with the heaviest of hearts and had no philosophical thoughts whatsoever for three weeks.

The worst thing about it all, said Papa, was that Kant began to sleep soundly at night.

'But isn't it good to sleep at night, Papa?' I asked.

'No, Minou, a philosopher should never sleep soundly.'

'But why?' I thought that sounded terrible. 'Don't you sleep, Papa?'

'My girl, that is my greatest sorrow, I drink coffee every night and yet I sleep like a bear in hibernation.' Papa's cheeks flushed. 'As if there was nothing to work out, no problems at all.'

I thought of my nights awake in the lighthouse and all the scarves I had knitted after Mama disappeared, and I wondered if staying up at night had made me a better philosopher.

Papa claimed the first word I said was 'Hegel'. Mama said that I had just eaten my first enormous portion of stewed apples and had the hiccups.

But Papa insisted. 'You had such an intelligent

look in your eyes, Minou. You looked straight at me and said "Hegel", loud and clear. And,' he lowered his voice, 'I read Hegel's *Phenomenology of Spirit* to you when you were still in your mama's womb. She thinks his sentences are too long, Minou, but I read to you while she was asleep. So you see, it's perfectly plausible that your first word would be "Hegel".'

I read Descartes' *Meditations* when I was ten, and tried to read Kant's *Critique of Pure Reason*, but couldn't make anything of it. Then I read Galileo and Freud. Freud, Papa explained, wasn't really a philosopher, but still part of modern thinking.

'You have to know what is out there,' he said. 'The more you know, Minou, the more equipped you are to find the truth.'

But Descartes wasn't just a great philosopher, said Papa. He was also our ancestor and it was therefore especially important to know his philosophy well.

Papa told me that Descartes' first name was René and that he was born in France on a cold day in March 1596.

Descartes said, 'I think, therefore I am.' He argued that it is only through thinking that we can know something to be true.

I wasn't sure I completely understood, and asked Papa, 'You mean, we can't even know the ocean exists just by seeing it?'

'That's true Minou, we can't, although—,' he glanced through the window at the dark ever-changing sea, '—it makes for such a convincing argument that I am almost tempted to make an exception.'

'And me, Papa?'

'You?'

'Do I exist?'

'You definitely exist, can't you hear yourself think?'

'Yes, but you can't.'

Papa looked worried. 'I'll take your word for it,' he said, and patted my head as if to make quite sure I was really there.

A philosopher, Papa explained, spends most of his time searching the dark room of his mind for the absolute truth; the one he has no reason whatsoever to doubt. Grandfather once said to Papa, 'When you find the absolute truth it's like finding the beginning. It's like a string. You pull and pull and pull some more. And then it all falls into place.'

Papa hadn't found the beginning yet. But he had

found smaller truths, and taught me how to write them down:

> Truth:
> Theodora had great stamina.
>
> Evidence:
> 1) She built the houses and the church on the island.
> 2) She lived on the island with only a goat for company.
> 3) She read Aristotle every day.
>
> Deduction:
> Reason conquers all.

Papa often said that if only he had been as smart as Grandfather then he would have found the absolute truth a long time ago.

Kant still lay next to my pile of blankets in the lighthouse, and some nights I tried to decipher a sentence by torchlight. But all I could make out were odd shapes in the hollow spaces between the words: birds, lions, and the curve of Mama's rowboat that had lain near the fishing spot since the day she arrived.

***

It was the twenty-seventh scarf that I had knitted. Descartes too had a hobby. He loved parades and would travel far and wide to attend one. Papa said it was entirely possible that Descartes' hobby had contributed favourably to his reasoning. He encouraged me to keep knitting, so that I too could strengthen my philosophical faculties.

I glanced at the four portraits of Descartes on the big bulb. It was the same portrait, but in different sizes. I could barely make out his profile in the darkness, but I knew he looked both serious and brooding, as though he was pondering a very tricky philosophical question. Papa said I resembled Descartes quite a bit. I couldn't really see it; instead his sharp nose and his dark eyes reminded me of Peacock.

Papa was still talking downstairs. A hoarse cry from a raven cut through the night. Snow whirled and danced on every side of the lighthouse and Boxman had moved on to a slow tune on the accordion. I stopped knitting and measured the scarf. It reached from one end of the mattress to the other. It was almost finished.

Mama liked birds. She liked the blue-black feathers of the ravens and their strong beaks, and she had done many drawings of them. But the bird she liked more than any other was Peacock.

When Mama arrived she opened her red suitcase and unpacked five dresses, eight jars of paint, two brushes and a white enamel clock that didn't work. She left the golden bowl outside the house, wherein Peacock immediately settled. Mama warned Papa that Peacock had seen things during the war that no bird should see. He had become sensitive and was known to nip without rhyme or reason. Papa didn't know much about birds, but he knew how to repair clocks, and asked if Mama wanted hers fixed. But she didn't, she liked time standing perfectly still.

Peacock lay in the golden bowl for hours each day, head resting lazily on the edge, but when he died years later, the golden bowl got filled with rain and snow, and over time it lost its shine. Mama didn't like the bowl without Peacock in it. She even kicked it one day, because it reminded her that he had died. The bowl rolled onto its side where it lay, grey and neglected. But that didn't stop the boatmen wanting to buy it.

The boatmen came with our weekly deliveries. We would all be on the beach, Papa and me, Boxman,

Mama and Priest, when their ship arrived out past the reef. We would watch the boatmen lower a dinghy into the chaotic sea and hear them swear across the waves. They didn't like coming to the island. Our deliveries often consisted of packages in strange shapes and if they saw a box on the beach next to Boxman, packed and ready to go, then their swearing grew louder.

With every delivery the boatmen got a new shopping list. Mama used to add a list to Papa's weekly order:

Flowers, red (if not possible, then yellow)
Ink, black
Three boxes of Zackerburg's Ginger Treats (make sure it's not Tennille's Delights, they are too chewy)
Three tubes of oil paint: cerulean blue
A stuffed bird, white, to put in hair, not too big
Green ribbon
A pair of reading glasses. Same as the previous pair
A box of oranges, the finest you can get
A paintbrush, 15mm, horsehair only
Four rolls of violet yarn and another pair of knitting needles for Minou

The boatmen had lined faces and thin mouths, and their eyes were watery blue. They lived on the ship and whenever they had to step onto the beach they looked uncomfortable and wobbly, as if the sea moved inside them.

Once their dinghy capsized as it was leaving the island with one of Boxman's wrapped boxes. Boxman shouted, the boatmen got wet and the box was lost. The sea was very deep. A few metres out the sand abruptly gave way to an oceanic grave, six hundred and fifty metres deep. The box for Ludwig von Bundig, Master of Card and Magic Tricks, sank to the bottom. I hoped it had lost its lid on the way down. It would make an extravagant home for fish and the kind of one-eyed creatures that live in the darkest places of the sea.

But, a few weeks later, Boxman's loss was made up for in the unexpected form of No Name. The boatmen had no idea they had a dog on board. It was only when they lowered their dinghy into the sea that No Name appeared, jumping in one daring leap to sit between them. As they reached the shore, and before any of us knew what was happening, No Name scrambled onto the sand and ran straight past us, up the path.

When Boxman arrived home, No Name was sitting in the lilac interior of a spare box. Boxman wasn't happy; he had never wanted a dog and certainly not a dog in one of his boxes. But later I found them: No Name asleep in the box, little dream-feet moving against the satin, and next to him Boxman, tenderly watching.

Papa was asleep when the boatmen stumbled across the golden bowl. He had spent all night having nightmares about the cellar, and the boatmen had agreed to help Mama and me up the path with the deliveries. When they saw the bowl, abandoned and dirty in front of the house, they wanted to buy it.

Mama wanted nothing of their proposals, not even when they offered her a special blue paint from France. And when they kept insisting she got angry.

'Go back to your boat and find yourself some manners,' she said.

I stood next to Mama, keeping an eye on the boatmen, as they wobbled down the hill past Theodora's gates.

'But Mama, you don't really like that bowl,' I said, as we watched them get back in their dinghy and leave the island.

'It's there to remind me.'

'Of what?'

'Two friends that survived the unspeakable.' Mama turned around and walked towards the house.

'What happened in the war, Mama?' I ran after her. 'With you and Peacock?'

'Don't ask me that again, Minou.' Mama stopped at the doorstep to pin up a strand of her hair. 'You know I can't talk about it.' Then she opened the door and went inside.

It was very late when I finished the scarf. Boxman had stopped playing and the lights in his barn were out. I folded the scarf, buried myself in the blankets and closed my eyes. I fell asleep listening to Papa's voice and thinking about the ravens. How surprised they must have been all those years ago, when they flew out towards Mama's rowboat, like twirling, tumbling hats, and saw Peacock sitting in the golden bowl.

Papa was rummaging through a drawer when I came downstairs the next morning. A gust of snow followed me through the front door into the warm kitchen. Papa was wearing an old fur hat, and gave me a rare smile as I stamped my boots free of snow on the mat.

'It's extraordinary, Minou,' he said, pulling a knife from the drawer as if he had just found a wonderful treasure. 'I feel young and invigorated.'

'Why, Papa?' I sat down at the kitchen table, noticing that Papa did in fact look different.

'I am close to finding the beginning, Minou. The first truth.' Papa poured me a coffee and began to slice the bread vigorously. 'Ah, if only your mama were here. There are so many things I would like to tell her, Minou.'

'What would you say to her, Papa?' I asked eagerly.

'Oh, it's very exciting.' Papa put two pieces of bread on my plate, and pushed the butter and jam closer to me. 'First, of course, I would tell her that with a constant temperature of six degrees below zero the dead boy is keeping remarkably fresh.' Papa fumbled in his pocket and withdrew a crumpled note. 'I measured the temperature at precise intervals last night, Minou.' He waved the note in front of me. 'But there is something else. In the middle of the night, as I was speaking to the dead boy, I saw his face in the shadows. His jaw, his hair, and I realised—' Papa paused for effect, '—that he looks distinctly like a young Descartes.' He took a gulp of coffee. 'How strange we didn't notice that yesterday, Minou.'

I buttered my bread and watched Papa retrieve his bucket from the cupboard. He seemed to have forgotten what Mama liked. He seemed to have forgotten that she believed in the imagination, and not in Descartes or measurements at precise intervals.

* * *

Once Mama closed her eyes and let her hand run through No Name's fur. 'Try, Minou,' she said, 'tell me what he feels like.'

No Name looked slightly confused, scarf askew, but I closed my eyes and felt his fur.

'Like a pinecone?' I said, then blushed, feeling I had spoken without thinking.

'A pinecone?' said Mama, and nodded as if I had just done something special.

Mama said she could feel snow, little cold shapes in her body, two days before it arrived.

Most times she was right. But Papa said that, if you say something often enough, you are sure to be right once in a while, and it did snow a lot on the island. And besides, Mama's predictions often seemed to change with the way she was feeling.

'Did you know, Minou,' she said one day, 'that seafarers and explorers of all kinds have visited this island? She looked out at the horizon. 'I can see them arrive!'

'Who, Mama?'

'A pirate and his men, Minou, on a huge black ship. There is surf spraying from the bow and there, right there,' Mama pointed, 'is a silverfin tuna. It's jumping alongside their ship.'

'Were there silverfin tuna then too, Mama?'

'Oh yes, Minou, there have always been silverfin tuna. This is a wonderful place. We are surrounded by history, little one.'

I stared in the same direction as Mama, but saw nothing apart from the endless sea, not even the faintest outline of a pirate.

But on another day Mama said, 'This is a terrible, terrible place, Minou,' shaking her head in despair. 'No one can live on this island and stay sane. Not even Theodora, with her big hands and her "Reason conquers all".'

'But she did live here,' I said.

'She died.'

'That was an accident,' I protested.

'That,' said Mama, 'is what everyone wants us to believe, little one.'

'What do you mean, Mama?'

'I mean that reason doesn't help much when you are stranded on a barren island.'

A few days before I was born Mama found a black fish. It was beating its tail in the shallow water of a rock pool. Sea salt glittered like small stars on its scaly body, the way, she later told me, that things become bright and visible when something extraordinary is about to happen. Mama had wrapped her scarf around the fish and was going to cook it for dinner. But halfway home, just before the gates, the fish cried out. It was a terrible cry, and as she unwrapped it, it looked straight at her, still crying out, its mouth wide open. It cried out like a cat, a baby, a siren, a rusty pipe, and all of them at once.

After that Mama wanted nothing to do with the fish, but Papa examined it and declared it to be a fine, healthy specimen and fried it for dinner. For the next two days he was sick in bed. Fever coursed through his body, and he couldn't stop thinking about the root cellar. The war, he said, was in his blood again.

I was born three days later, and Mama was certain things would have gone very differently if she had listened to Papa and eaten the fish.

Everyone knew the story of my birth. Priest said, 'Your mama was bigger than the church bell, Minou. Every night when I got to bed, I would look at the bell and pray for a safe delivery.'

Even Boxman, who had come to the island years later, would say, 'That fish was scary, Minou.

Your mama trembled like an actress before the final curtain call.'

I asked Mama to tell the story of my birth again and again. And she never said no.

'I was walking on the beach, right near the spot where I found the dead fish, when I suddenly felt an odd pain in my finger.' Mama would hold up her left index finger and look at it curiously. 'And the pain didn't stop. It got worse. I sat down on a rock near the fishing spot and noticed that the ocean was unnaturally quiet. It was blank, like a sheet of drawing paper. And then the pain in my finger shot straight into my stomach. It wasn't just pain, Minou, it felt like the waves had moved from the sea and into me. Soon I didn't know whether it was me yelling, or if it was the cry of the fish still hanging in the air. When Priest found me I was lying on the sand and you were almost there.'

'Did Priest get scared, Mama?'

'No,' Mama shook her head. 'No, he was the finest helper. He put his jacket under me and he held my hand and I remember his eyes, Minou. He looked at me in the kindest way. I kept telling him that the fish was a bad omen and that I could still hear it crying out. But Priest kept saying, "I have it on good authority that it will be a girl and that she will be a blessing to us all."' Mama looked at me. 'I remember everything he said. He talked about pretzels and God, it was good to hear his voice.'

'What happened then, Mama?'

'You were born on Priest's coat right at the water's edge. And just as you arrived, your Papa came running down the path. He sat down in the water at my feet and took you in his arms. You were tiny, Minou, with the darkest hair.'

'What did Papa say?'

'He didn't say much, little one. He was just so happy to see you. He kissed you and held you as if he had always had a little girl to look after. And then the ocean started moving again, one wave after another and you, little one, you stared into the sea like you knew it well. Then you looked at us in turn, at your Papa, at Priest and at me. And your Papa was sure that it was your way of saying hello to all of us.'

Papa was glad that Mama didn't eat any of the fish. But even though she was right about the fish, he insisted that in general there is only one way to the truth and that is Descartes' way.

***

I put jam on my bread and watched Papa as he buttoned up his coat, and got his nets and bucket ready. I needed to remind him what kind of things Mama liked. But it was difficult. Papa never wanted to talk about her. Like everyone else on the island, he was convinced she was dead.

I thought she was dead, too, right at the beginning. I even told No Name that she had been swallowed by a great big whale beneath Theodora's Plateau, one dark eye peering from below the surface of the water.

No Name looked as if he didn't quite believe me, but I reminded him of the story of Jonah, and that Mama, with her long red hair and black umbrella, would have caught any whale's eye, and that she always, always, walked too close to the edge.

Mama disappeared the morning after the circus performance.

We had rehearsed for weeks, Mama, Boxman and I. Mama had put a big cross in the calendar for the day of the circus, and Papa and Priest had each received an invitation that she had expertly composed, sitting on a bale of hay in Boxman's barn with an old black typewriter on her lap.

Come to the circus!

Time: 6pm Saturday

Place: Boxman's Barn

Dress: marvellously

Prepare to be surprised

A storm reached the island some hours after the circus performance. I had watched from the tower as wind moved sand and pebbles from one end of the beach to the other. Lightning lit up the sky and Priest had rung the church bell until it was all over.

By morning the storm had passed and the rain was falling softly.

Papa had stayed in bed and left the fish to their own devices, and Turtle, who was blind and lived under the doorstep, appeared in the kitchen next to the stove. Turtle didn't venture inside very often, and Mama almost stepped on him while making breakfast. His shell was wet and he looked like a different turtle.

'He is so shiny,' I said. 'He is the same colour as the curtain last night, Mama. At the circus.'

Mama didn't reply. Instead she paused behind me to smooth the collar of my dress. I had to wear a dress every day and didn't like it. I preferred wearing pants and a big green jumper with deep pockets, useful for storing things found on the beach. But every morning Mama would say, 'Something special might happen today, Minou. And then you would want to be dressed for the occasion.'

The morning Mama disappeared she sat down on the edge of a kitchen chair and looked at me from across the table.

'You should put your hair up, little one,' she said, leaning over crumbs and coffee cups to tuck a strand of hair behind my ear.

Her eyes were a darker grey than normal. She looked tired. The door to the blue room was open when I got up. There was a blanket at the end of the bed. And I wondered if Mama had slept there instead of with Papa.

I shook my head. 'I am going to visit Priest.'

Mama got back up and started to wipe the kitchen bench.

'It falls down when I run,' I explained.

Turtle headed towards the living room, almost hitting the door.

'Will he be able to find his way out?' I asked, feeling sorry for him.

Mama didn't answer. She took off her apron and placed it on the chair. Then she picked out her purple shoes from the rack—her actress shoes she called them—with heels and a flower sewn on the side, and put them on.

I could see the ocean through the open kitchen door. A paint tin that must have belonged to Boxman floated on the quiet sea. I thought of how Priest had rung the bell, and how frightened he must have been by the storm.

'Poor Priest,' I said.

It was what Mama usually said when we saw the church lit up like a ship on a stormy night.

'Yes.' She stroked my cheek and smiled a sad kind of smile. 'Poor Priest.' Then she picked up Turtle and a black umbrella and walked out into the rain. I could see her walk down the path with the umbrella held high, stepping around the gates, then, swaying slightly in her heels, reaching the beach.

Papa appeared, standing in an old singlet, looking at the open door and then at Mama's coffee cup on the table, still full.

'Why is the door open, Minou?'

'Mama has gone for a walk.'

Papa poured himself a coffee. He looked tired. 'Is she all right?'

'Yes, Papa.'

I kept looking at Mama in the distance, mesmerised by her silhouette, partly obscured by the black umbrella. But afterwards I couldn't remember the last moment I saw her or where she was on the beach. It was like the vanishing act Mama had performed with Boxman the night before. One moment she was there, the next she wasn't. All I remembered was the swaying of her umbrella.

Later that afternoon we searched for Mama. We searched the beach and Theodora's Plateau. Boxman turned his barn upside down; he looked behind the apothecary's desk and inside every box. And we searched the church. Papa climbed the stairs to the tower, but found nothing apart from Priest's bed and the large silent bell. I looked in the shed next to the church, but I already knew there wasn't room for anything else but the rusty machine. Priest even opened the door to his industrial oven.

The rain turned to snow then back to rain and late afternoon we went back to our house, all terribly wet and cold.

That night we waited up, sitting around the

kitchen table. No Name slept next to the oven, and Priest, who was fond of origami, folded an enormous number of paper cranes.

'Cranes are such graceful animals, don't you think, Minou? They remind me of your mama,' he said, his hands working incessantly.

Papa didn't say much. He made coffee over and over, and seemed to forget his manners when Boxman started crying and told us that Mama was by far the best circus artist he had ever worked with, better even than Cosmina.

Boxman turned to Priest, 'Remember last night? The way she sang?'

Priest nodded. 'She was spectacular.'

Boxman blew his nose on a serviette, 'A real circus princess. The flower in her...'

Papa banged the coffeepot down onto the table so hard that the coffee spilled over and burnt his hand. 'There will be no mention of the circus tonight.'

'But Papa,' I said.

'Not even from you, Minou.'

Boxman went home early, but left No Name for me to look after. Priest stayed and told Papa about Moses. But I don't think Papa listened. He just sat listlessly, staring into an empty cup as Priest recounted Moses' extraordinary strength in the face of trying circumstances.

I woke on the floor at dawn, certain that a boat horn had droned somewhere far away. I lay listening, waiting for the horn to sound again, but it didn't. No Name was sleeping, warm against me. At some stage during the night Papa must have covered us with a blanket. Priest was asleep at the table, and over the chair next to him hung Mama's apron. Papa moved around the kitchen, clearing the table and making a new batch of coffee.

That morning I expected Mama to walk through the front door, put on her apron and say, 'I am home, little one.' But she didn't. It was only later that day that I realised Turtle had disappeared as well.

Papa thought that a wind, unusually strong, had swept like a rope around Mama's legs and dragged her over the edge of Theodora's Plateau.

'There are times,' he explained, his voice low and sad, 'when the wind blows, fast and high, travelling much faster than you and I can run. When that happens not even an umbrella can temper the fall. There is nothing you can do but to spread your arms and let yourself be carried out.'

A few days after Mama disappeared I went to

visit Boxman. I was almost at his yard when I heard crying. I looked between the trees, and saw Boxman hunched over on a bale of hay. Priest was sitting next to him, patting him on the back.

'She has walked into the ocean, I know it.' Boxman wiped his eyes with a square of green silk lining from one of his boxes.

'Now, now. I don't think so,' said Priest. 'It was an accident. She loved everyone too much to do such a thing.'

'But you don't understand. The vanishing act changes people. I kept saying it to her.'

'One circus trick more or less wouldn't make any difference, dear Boxman. It was all just light-hearted fun.'

But Boxman didn't seem to hear Priest. 'She promised me that she wasn't going to change. But remember, Priest, I have seen it all before.' Boxman started sobbing again.

I don't think No Name liked hearing Boxman cry. He sat in the middle of the yard, scratching himself, looking mournful. And when I turned around and walked back along the forest path he came running after me.

We went to the beach. The sky was full of rain and

almost as dark as the sea. The horizon was blurred. No Name bounced ahead of me, running through the wet sand. We reached Theodora's Plateau and went to the edge and looked into the dark, crashing waves below. As we stood there, gazing into the sea, No Name started howling. He howled and howled, his body shaking. And I stood next to him, about to cry. 'Don't, No Name,' I whispered. 'Please don't.' But No Name didn't listen. He kept howling, staring shakily into the waves below. Then I couldn't stand it any longer. I picked him up harder than I wanted to and carried him back to Boxman.

Two months later Priest found one of Mama's shoes on the beach. Papa was standing on a box in the study looking for Spinoza's *Tractatus de Intellectus Emendatione* on top of the bookshelf, when we heard shouting from the beach in what sounded like another language. Papa ran out the door without even stopping to put on shoes. Halfway down the path, he turned and called out to me that I was under no circumstances to follow him.

'What language did you speak?' I later asked Priest.

'I can't remember,' he said. 'It was as if the whole

world was in my throat. It could have been any language, Minou, any language at all.'

I soon realised that everyone was being dramatic, and that I had been both silly and childish to think that a whale could have swallowed Mama. I sat No Name down once more, made sure he was listening and told him that whales on the whole are innocent creatures and that I didn't know what had come over me. I told him that, because I was the only one on the island thinking in a rational manner, it was up to me to prove that Mama was still alive and to find her. I wrote in my notebook:

> Everyone believes that you are dead, Mama. But I don't think so.
>
> Papa says that the wind swept you over Theodora's Plateau.
>
> Priest found one of your shoes today. I hope that you can buy another pair where you are now.
>
> We all miss you.

I asked Papa to help me look in Mama's old atlas, so we could work out where she had gone. But Papa said that her red suitcase was still in her room and if she had gone anywhere she would have taken it with her. And when I tried to convince Papa that maybe she just wanted a new suitcase he said that it wasn't logical. She already had one that was perfectly good and sturdy.

But I thought of all the peculiar things I had read about, things that didn't make sense. I told Papa of whole cities under water, streets filled with drifting seaweed and glittering fish, and I told him of the enormous overweight octopus they caught in the ocean, that had jumped straight from the ship's scales back to the water, just after registering two-and-a-half tonnes. When all that was possible then surely it was also possible that Mama had left without her suitcase and would be coming back soon. But Papa didn't listen.

I was disappointed in Papa. It was as if he had forgotten everything he had taught me about finding the truth in the darkness of your mind. I could almost hear Descartes exclaim, 'As if a shoe is prrroooff of anything!'

I stood in the doorway as Papa left for his fishing spot. It was the morning after I found the dead boy. The island was hazily lit by the grey morning light. Frost stung my face as I watched him walk down the path with a spring in his step.

By the time Papa reached the gates I regretted not going with him. The blue room was cold and I didn't feel like drawing the dead boy. But Papa had always told me that logic never changes, never bends, and that it can be held like a shield against anything daunting: snowstorms, bad weather and years without apples on the apple tree.

I went back to the kitchen table, opened my notebook, and turned to my argument for Mama being alive. I had written the argument on the day of the shoe funeral, the day before Uncle came to visit. I was proud of it. It was logically sound and written in my neatest handwriting. Papa always said that order is a philosopher's best friend. Without order, he said, you cannot convince anyone of anything. And I wanted to prove to Uncle that Mama was still alive. Being an academic and therefore a rational thinking man, I needed him to help me persuade everyone that Mama was coming back.

I poured myself another coffee and read the argument out loud, as I had done many times before.

Argument for Mama being alive:

1) Things that disappear on an island are always found. For example:

Mama's shopping list—found
Tin of dog food—found
Tobacco—found
A blue enamel jug for milk—found, minus the milk
My yellow soft socks—found (very dirty)
Papa's matches—found
No Name—found, hurt

I often reminded No Name of the day he disappeared. He looked at me as if he remembered clearly how the delivery ship had come and gone and how it had taken a long time to load one of Boxman's boxes. Papa had thought that No Name might have jumped into the dinghy and left the island the same way he had come. Boxman looked at the ship, a tiny dot on the horizon, and did a half wave.

But Mama got that unseeing look in her eyes and said, 'He hasn't gone. He is here, I can feel it.'

Later we found him on the beach, shivering behind a large rock, a shard of sea glass stuck in his paw.

2) Things lost to the ocean always return.

Things lost to the ocean returned without fail, getting caught in the arms of rocks and whitened pine branches. Although odd things sometimes washed up on the beach, such as the violin and the bike with the bent rusty wheels, it didn't change the fact that when things left the island they always came back.

Papa had told me it was to do with the reef. Once he forgot to take off his reading glasses before he went fishing and dropped them into the sea. Before he knew it they were washed out. I found them on the other side of the island two days later with one lens broken. Another time Mama put a letter in a bottle, sealed it with a cork and, standing on Theodora's Plateau, wind pulling at her dress, she threw it out as far as she could. After five weeks it returned near the fishing spot. The letter said: 'Help me, I am trapped on an island in the middle of the sea.'

'Poor woman,' laughed Mama, and put the note back in the bottle.

It was clear to me that Mama was neither on the island, nor in the sea, and, although Descartes might not have liked it, I included Turtle and Cosmina in my list of evidence. If Mama had decided to walk into the ocean the way Boxman said, she would never have taken Turtle with her. And if the vanishing act had made Cosmina want to travel, then it might have done the same to Mama. Finally I added her purple shoes as extra evidence. Normally she didn't wear her actress shoes to the beach, but in that area Mama was a bit unpredictable.

The more I thought about it the more I knew it to be true. Mama was still alive. And I wished that everyone would stop looking so sad when I mentioned her. But one night, sitting in the tower, watching a storm, I thought I heard singing. First I thought it was the silverfin tuna or maybe the cries of whales. The voice was mournful. As if it had been locked in a bottle for hundreds of years and suddenly escaped; a genie calling out, mourning all that she didn't get to do, all the beautiful things she didn't get to see.

But the song had words, lines that were repeated again and again: 'There is a song, there is a sea, goodbye to the man who waits for me.'

I sat still. At every lightning bolt I looked out, searching the island for any sign of where the voice might be coming from. And there, in a bright flash, I saw Mama's black umbrella, pulled and pushed by rain and wind along the beach and into the water.

Suddenly it was the loneliest night, and it was Mama's voice, and it was the saddest song I had ever heard. It sounded as if she was singing from the depths of the frozen sea. My breath was not my own and everything felt wrong. The island felt as if it was going to tip at any time and rush us all into the sea.

Scared that Papa might hear it too, I got up from my blankets and ran downstairs. But Papa looked up from his book and smiled when I found him in the study, and everything was quiet. I didn't tell him about the voice. Instead I sat down and drew the umbrella for Mama. I drew it upside down, illuminated by a flash of lightning, as Papa read to me from Descartes' *Meditations.*

'You have to start,' he read, 'with the simplest truth, the fundamental truth of which there can be no doubt, followed by the truths deduced from them, going from simple to more complex.' With Descartes' words the island became solid again and I realised how easily logic gets lost in the night.

I reread my truths again and again and couldn't find anything wrong with them and I didn't think that Descartes would have either.

My next step was to work out where Mama might have gone. But it was difficult. Mama liked things to do with the imagination, while Papa and I were philosophers. Papa often said that it was difficult for a philosopher to know what Mama liked and what she wanted. When we saw her walk along the beach, singing loudly, her hair pulled by wind and sea salt, Papa would look at me and say, 'When there is something you don't understand, Minou, then you have to research the problem, approach it with logic.'

Papa had been gone for a while. It was time to

see the dead boy. I put my plate in the sink, got my notebook and an extra scarf and went to the blue room.

The raven sat in the open window, unblinking in the bleak morning light. I could just make out Mama on the wall, smiling and waving.

Papa had placed an armchair right next to the bed. Beside it stood the wobbly lamp we normally used in the kitchen. There was a blanket on the chair and Papa's empty cup sat nearby. More snow had collected on the floor overnight and the dead boy looked very cold. I pulled the chair back, sat down and tried to do what Mama had taught me. 'Rule number one,' she used to say, 'lift your pencil only after observing.'

His jacket bulked around his chest; it was frozen and salt-stained. Studying him I wondered if anyone had heard his last words and if they had been important. There was sand in his hair and on the bed, but I was sure that Mama wouldn't mind. She only used the bed when she was daydreaming. Then she would lie with closed eyes, her shoes pointing to the ceiling like little boats.

'It's important to daydream, Minou,' she would say, her hair spilling over the pillow. 'It's important to let your mind travel, and not hold it tight like a dog on a leash.'

'A dog of war, Mama?'

'*Any* kind of dog, Minou.'

I chose a coloured pencil and tried to think in curious ways. I drew the salt pattern on his jacket and wrote, 'The salt looks like flowers.'

'What kind of flowers?' Mama would ask, sitting at the kitchen table, waiting for Papa to make her a coffee with lots of cream and sugar. 'What did they look like, Minou?'

'Sea lilies.'

'Really?' she would say. 'What else?'

'Oranges,' I would add.

'Oranges?'

And Papa would look up from the kitchen bench and say, in a very interesting manner, 'He smelled of oranges.'

'How peculiar,' Mama would reply. 'A dead boy smelling of oranges.'

Papa would forget about philosophy and say, 'I talked to him all night, didn't sleep a wink.'

And Mama would arrange her long hair in a loose bun, and look thoughtful and happy.

* * *

I drew the dead boy's bare foot. I took my time, and paid extra attention to his black toenails. Then I drew the shoe on the floor, the flimsy pale-blue scarf around his neck and noticed that one of the buttons on his jacket was gold, while the rest were brown. I tried to draw the gold button too, but it was hard to copy the way it sparkled in the light of the lamp.

I could see the dead boy's ear through matted hair. It was dark grey, almost like the smoke from our chimney.

It felt like he was listening.

I waited for a moment, then whispered, 'I have a secret, dead boy.'

And it wasn't just that his ear was grey, it was something else. I was certain that he wanted to hear my secret.

'What was it like sitting next to the dead boy?' Mama would ask.

'As if he could hear me.'

'Hear what?'

'The pencils, my drawing. As if he was listening,' I said.

'Listening?'

'Like Priest in the confession box.'

Mama didn't like religion. 'All those rules and regulations,' she would say when I got ready for church on Sundays. 'They got it all wrong,' she would shout as I ran out the door to pick up No Name before the bell rang across the island. But, even though Mama didn't like religion, she still enjoyed visiting Priest. She admired the church paintings and sometimes she even liked a story from the Bible. She had planned to paint all the animals from Noah's ark, starting from the back of the house running along every wall until she reached the front door.

'It's going to look as if they have just arrived at Mount Ararat, and are filing out, two by two, to look at the sun,' she said.

Papa didn't mind that I was going to church. The Bible, he said, is an historical document and useful to know.

'Just remember, Minou,' he said, 'most people do not separate God from expectation.' He peered at me over his reading glasses. 'It's important that you understand this. Expectation has no place in thought. People want something for their faith; they want something for their prayers. They are bargaining with God. But philosophy is a pursuit of truth, and that is,' he emphasised, 'truth without expectation.'

After Mama disappeared I started bringing my notebook to church. Every Sunday Priest would speak from the pulpit with conviction and address, not just No Name and me, but the whole church with all its empty pews. He would fold origami while he talked about the creation of the world, sending swans, cats, flowers, cranes and buffaloes, his specialty, down the nave. Some of them, often the ones with wings, would glide gracefully to the floor.

No Name loved origami and howled every time a piece left the pulpit. I liked origami too, and I liked Genesis, except for one bit. Every time Priest got to the part about darkness covering the surface of the deep I got scared. And ever since Mama disappeared I thought it was the scariest thing of all; the deep with only a layer of darkness to prevent anyone from falling in. It reminded me of ocean graves hiding ships of moaning wood, hiding things long forgotten, and, against all logic, I kept seeing Mama's red hair fanning out, pulling down, deeper and deeper.

The dark-panelled confession box sat at the back of the church beside the stairs that led to the tower. It had plum-coloured curtains that dragged, tired and dusty, on the floor. Once, when Priest asked me if I wanted to do confession, I stepped inside and sat down with No Name on my lap. I could hear Priest behind the flower-carved partition.

'What am I supposed to say?' I asked.

'Tell me whatever sins you have committed; entrust me with them,' he answered. 'It's quite straightforward.'

I moved uncertainly on the velvet-covered bench. 'I don't really know what a sin is,' I said, feeling that this was a serious flaw after all the philosophy I had been reading.

'Things you might have done wrong, secrets you haven't told another soul,' said Priest.

And right then I almost told Priest what had happened the night of the circus. But I stopped myself and told him instead that I very much wanted a horse. It wasn't really a secret and I didn't think it was a sin either, but Priest listened as I told him all I knew about horses while stroking the coarse hair on No Name's back.

I told Priest that getting a horse to the island

wouldn't be easy. A horse would have to withstand the sea journey. It would have to be lowered with leather straps from the ship into the water and then swim behind the dinghy until it reached the shore.

The boatmen wouldn't be happy and the whole thing was enough to scare any horse out of its wits, said Papa. In fact, it might not have any wits left by the time it reached the island.

'Horses are sensitive creatures,' nodded Priest.

I thought both Priest and Papa underestimated horses, and it was a small strong horse I wanted anyway, with a mind of its own.

I imagined bringing Mama to the tower on her first day home, saying, 'Look Mama, try and find something new.' She would gaze, first in one direction, then in another, and suddenly spot the horse behind the forest, running wherever it pleased.

'Is there anything else you want to tell me?' Priest asked in a kind voice.

Again I almost told him about standing in Boxman's yard after the circus, about how it had rained softly, and about the strange sound I had heard. But this time I pulled the curtain open and swung my legs around so I sat sideways. No Name jumped to the floor and Priest appeared next to me.

We sat there side by side as if in a little boat, blinded for a moment by the many coloured lights that fell from Theodora's window. Priest had been preaching in his chef's outfit and the smell of pretzels spread through the church like a salty wave. Just that morning he had received twenty bags of flour from the boatmen and ten new baking trays that shone like silver. It had taken three trips with the wheelbarrow to deliver it all to his kitchen.

'Who pays you to be a priest?' I asked.

'My parents had lots of money,' he said. 'They died and left it all to me.' He pulled out a piece of origami paper from his apron and started folding it. 'They weren't nice people; they didn't believe in God.'

I thought of Papa who didn't believe in God either, but was kind and had invited Mama for tea when she was just a stranger with tangled hair.

'Maybe they believed in something else,' I suggested, thinking they might have searched for truth without expectation just like Papa.

'Pigs,' he said, 'they believed in pigs. They had a barn with hundreds and hundreds of them.'

'Pigs are lovely,' I said politely. 'They have soft ears.'

Priest didn't look like he cared for soft ears.

'They slept in the barn. Under a big tartan blanket.'

'The pigs?'

'No, my parents.' Priest looked unhappy.

'But where did you sleep?'

'In the house, Minou. But talking about this brings up bad memories. It was so quiet at night, not a sound, and it was always dark. Pigs don't like light, you see. Not even when it comes from across the yard.' He looked at me. 'Promise me, Minou, that you will never get a pig.'

'I don't think I will,' I said. 'I really want a horse.'

'Horses are nice,' said Priest.

I still hadn't convinced Papa that I needed a horse. Every time I asked he said, 'You have two feet and can run very fast. Probably faster, Minou, than a horse.'

I picked up the dead boy's shoe from the floor of the blue room. I didn't tell him my secret. Instead I wondered what had happened to him. The shoe was cold and greasy with salt. I looked down at my own boots. They were getting too small, squeezing against my toes when I ran. Mama had ordered them from the boatmen, but first she made me stand on a piece of paper in the kitchen so she could trace the shape of my feet. Before handing the sheet to the boatmen she decorated her drawing of my feet with palm trees, roses and a pelican busy swallowing a large and frightened fish.

We called for Papa to come and see her drawing. After studying it intently he told Mama that he liked it very much, especially the fish.

Mama laughed. 'But why the fish? It's getting eaten.'

'I know,' said Papa. 'But it has such lovely symmetry and its scales are all equal in size.'

And Mama put her arms around him and kissed him on the mouth for a long time. Papa blushed, but looked happy and patted me on the head a little too hard as he walked back to his study.

After he left, Mama grew serious. She studied the drawing. 'Your feet will take you many places, Minou,' she said, adding another line to the pelican. 'No one is destined to stay on one island alone. We all need to see at least three of the seven seas in our life time, little one.'

I couldn't imagine my feet taking me anywhere else but around the island, but I didn't tell her that.

* * *

By now it was getting light. The pine trees outside got their colour back, and the dead boy's ear looked more blue than grey. I noted in my book:

> The dead boy's ear is almost the same blue colour as Boxman's cape.
>
> There is a gold button on his jacket, Mama, and his hair is dark, almost as dark as mine.

I looked through my notes and drawings. I already had quite a few, but I was convinced that Mama would want to hear more. Papa had searched the dead boy's pockets, and hadn't found anything that could tell us who he was or where he was going. I looked at his gold button, thinking hard. Then I got the idea. I could write a story for Mama. About the dead boy. And I could give it to her when she came back.

I found a blank page in my notebook and began to write, with the shoe still in my lap.

> *The Curious and Interesting Story about a Boy.*
>
> *Once there was a dead boy. Before he died he travelled the seven seas on a large black ship. When*

he stood on the ship it felt as if he was flying. Surf sprayed from the bow and alongside the ship jumped a silverfin tuna.

It was Pirate's ship. Pirate also had a monkey, but she wasn't very nice. Her name was Monkey. She tried to bite anyone who came close. It was Pirate who rescued the boy, but not like rescuing him from a fire. Instead Pirate asked the boy, 'Do you want to see my ship?'

I paused, and read it out loud. The dead boy looked as if he liked the story, and when I glanced at Mama on the wall I felt certain that she would like it too. I sat for a moment pondering what Boxman might tell Mama if he knew about the dead boy. He was good at making up stories. Much better than me.

In the kitchen Papa's bucket rang hard against the floor. He was home. The raven, flapping wildly, left the windowsill and took refuge in the nearest pine tree, only to return a moment later.

I closed the notebook. I would read the boy his story when it was finished.

'There you are, my girl,' Papa said cheerfully, and winked at me in a way that made his face look all scrunched up and funny. He was busy hanging up the nets and in the middle of the floor sat the bucket, full of shiny black fish.

'Why are you back so early, Papa?'

'There is too much work to do.' Papa finished the nets, and stood back, inspecting them. Then he pulled off his boots. 'I didn't go on my philosopher's walk. Have you been sitting with the dead boy?'

'Yes, Papa.'

'Did you tell him about Descartes, Minou?' Papa put his boots next to the rack where Mama's shoes still sat in neat rows. 'I have covered quite a lot of it myself, but it never hurts to repeat the good bits. Although,' Papa said, 'I think there is a distinct possibility that he already knows about Descartes. He looks wise, doesn't he?'

'Maybe I can tell him about Uncle and how we are all related,' I suggested.

'Yes,' Papa agreed, 'sadly that's something most people don't know. There is nothing quite as melancholy as when historical facts are not acknowledged, don't you think, Minou?' Then he added, almost as an afterthought, 'He is in excellent condition, isn't he, my girl? Nice and frozen.'

No Name barked at the door and when Papa let him in he ran straight to the ice-cold oven and sniffed it with a whimper.

I picked him up and held him close to my chest. 'She is not here, No Name,' I whispered. 'But she is coming back.'

'Have you told Boxman about the dead boy?' Papa went to the fireplace and added more wood to the fire.

'Not yet, Papa.'

'Then you better go and see him now, my girl. The boatmen are coming the day after tomorrow. I don't think we will be able to straighten his knee.

Boxman might have to make a special box for him.'

Papa and Boxman hadn't spoken much since the shoe funeral. Boxman no longer came for coffee on the morning of the delivery boat, and Papa no longer waited on the beach with the rest of us, but instead collected his deliveries after Boxman had left. When I asked Papa why, he said, 'We just have different ways of doing things, my girl. There is nothing to worry about.'

Papa held the door for No Name and me as we left the house. 'Remember to tell Boxman about the dead boy,' Papa reminded me, as No Name and I left the house. 'Don't just play and forget about it.'

The morning was bright and white. No Name tumbled ahead of me as we went along the forest path. The pines stood tall and wide, their branches heavy with snow. Two rabbits crossed the path, but No Name didn't have time for them. He kept getting up on his hind legs, waving his front paws at the falling snow.

No Name was good at tricks—so good that Boxman was sure that he had performed before coming to the island. Boxman had written a letter to his old circus in Berlin, asking if they knew a dog with brown eyes and marvellous circus skills.

'It's very far to Berlin,' I said sceptically.

'Crazier things have happened,' said Boxman. 'No Name is a really special dog.'

Boxman asked me to do a drawing of No Name to accompany his letter and I drew him, daringly jumping through a burning hoop. It was the best picture I had ever done, and I wrote my name in the corner with a note politely asking the circus to return it.

No Name liked a lot of things. But he was especially fond of church on Sundays. He would bark when I brought him back, as if he were telling Boxman about all the exciting things that Priest had said.

Sometimes I wanted to tell Boxman about Priest's sermon too. Boxman liked everything to do with space. He had to keep up with all the new information, he said, in case Cosmina decided to come back from the Himalayas.

'When you love someone,' he said, 'it's important to be able to talk to her.'

One day, while Boxman was preparing tea in the corner, I read him the notes I had taken during the sermon, 'God made two good lights. The great light to govern the day and the lesser light to govern the night. He also made the stars.'

Boxman liked that, and wanted to know if Priest had said anything else about the stars. I shook my head and asked instead why he never came to church. Boxman answered that Priest's origami reminded him of Cosmina, and that sitting in church made him sad. She too had fidgety hands, he explained, and was always pulling apart pieces of paper.

'Bits and pieces would whirl around the house,' he said. 'Like snow and hail and rain. Later we would find paper in our tea, in the paint and in the honey.'

No Name took off when we got closer to the barn. He sprinted down the path and by the time I arrived he was already sitting next to Boxman, greeting me with a happy bark, as if he was surprised and delighted that I had come to visit.

Boxman was sandpapering the lid of a dark blue box, and the barn smelled deliciously of sawdust and paint. On the table sat the open box. A naked woman with large breasts was painted along the side. She had a whip in her mouth and smiled in a sort of uncomfortable way. 'La Luna' was written in large curly letters just above her breasts.

'Is that La Luna?' I asked, feeling the dry paint with my fingertips.

Boxman nodded, drawing his cape tighter against the cold.

'She looks brave.'

Boxman stepped back and looked at La Luna. 'She is not afraid of anything,' he said. 'You could take her to the darkest room at the end of the world and she still wouldn't be scared.'

Then Boxman asked me if I wanted to star in a trick. I nodded, but then felt nervous. I wasn't brave like La Luna.

'Take off your shoes,' he said. 'And lie still.'

I climbed into La Luna's box, notebook in hand.

'Sawing a woman in half is no funny business.' He paused at the lid. 'Do you need the notebook?' he asked.

I nodded.

'Right,' he said, 'let's get started.' Boxman took a deep breath, then called out in his circus voice, 'Ladies and Gentlemen! You are about to see a trick never before accomplished quite like this. Be prepared, be warned, watch every step, this is real, this is frightening, this is,' he declared, 'Minou, the Fearless!'

Boxman closed the lid with a flourish and I could no longer hear his voice. Darkness took over and I thought of God creating the world and the thin layer covering the deep. I held my breath and tried to act like Minou the Fearless, but felt instead that I was sinking deeper and deeper into a dark ocean, with Mother's hair, tentacles of red, reaching for me.

'Boxman,' I knocked on the lid. 'Let me out.'

When Boxman's face and the dusty ceiling appeared above me, I searched my mind for something to tell him that didn't involve La Luna.

'Do you think,' I asked, still lying down, with the notebook in my arms, 'that No Name knows how far it is to the church, just by looking at the bell tower?'

I had thought about this for quite some time and had saved it for one of our conversations. Even though Boxman wasn't a philosopher, he did know a lot about space.

Boxman lit a cigarette as I climbed out of the box. He had nice hands. They were always dotted with paint and he wore a gold ring on the right hand, set with a dark red stone.

I thought that he really shouldn't be smoking in the barn with all that hay lying around, and then wondered if he was disappointed in my circus performance.

'I don't know what he sees,' said Boxman, 'but I know what he hears. When the church bell rings, even if it's in the middle of the night, he waits for you at the door.'

It was true. No Name was always ready when I came to pick him up. He liked everything about church. Not just the sermons and Priest's origami, but also the church paintings that covered the walls and arched ceilings. He would stare at them enchanted throughout the service.

One morning when it was raining and Priest was doing his gymnastics inside, he told Mama and me that they were called frescoes.

'Frescoes tell stories,' he said, swinging his arms around in big circles. 'Stories about God.'

The largest, Mama's favourite, was of John the Baptist, painted in faded blues and reds. John was knee-deep in a river baptising a man amongst reeds and fish.

Priest stopped swinging his arms, pointed to John the Baptist, and said with conviction, 'God is in that painting, Minou. He is right there asking me to give him everything I have.'

'What do you mean, Priest?' I said. 'What does he ask for?'

'My life, Minou.' Priest smiled. 'My pretzels, my light bulbs, my origami, everything.'

'But where is he?' I asked, staring at the fresco.

'He is nowhere,' Mama said quite loudly, next to me. 'That painting, little one, is made up of magenta red and cobalt blue, and a great deal of artistic ability.'

Priest continued to talk as if he hadn't heard Mama. 'Look closely, Minou,' he said and began to walk on the spot, lifting his knees high. 'God is there,' he puffed. 'He is in the river, in the fish and in the man being baptised.'

I looked at the fresco, while listening to Priest, who exclaimed a loud 'wahh wahh uhh' on every knee-lift. The baptised man, head above water, looked surprised, as if he had seen the overweight octopus and the sunken city all at once. But, no matter how hard I looked, I couldn't see God and I wondered if No Name, sitting next to me, head side-ways, squinting at the fresco, might be seeing what I couldn't.

Just above the entrance to the church was a fresco of a large black dog, teeth glinting in a dangerous smile. He was dancing in a row of angels.

'That's the devil in disguise,' said Priest.

I thought it was silly of the devil to dress up as a black dog. But the angels seemed too busy dancing in their long flowing dresses to notice that they were holding hands with a dog. No Name, as if he knew perfectly well that the black dog wasn't who he pretended to be, would look suspiciously at the fresco every time we left the church.

A stained-glass window at the end of the church showed Theodora and her beloved goat next to the Apostle Paul. Theodora's hands were large. She held a brick in one and a paddle in the other, and looked big and strong next to Paul.

Priest often looked at Theodora with admiration. 'You wouldn't want to mess with her,' he said.

'Was she a real queen?' I asked.

'In a way she was,' he said. 'She wanted to be a queen so much that she bought the whole island and had her portrait painted.' Priest went into a deep back-bend, folding his hands awkwardly behind him, and added with a laboured voice, 'And she always wore a crown.'

Mama had found some of Priest's origami paper in the pulpit and was enthusiastically folding away. 'What a sad, lonely life. Sitting on a tiny island reading philosophy in the middle of nowhere.' Mama sent a crane that didn't seem to have any wings crashing to the floor. She looked out over the pews. 'This is like being at the wheel of a great big ship, isn't it?' she said.

'God's boat?' said Priest and added a 'wahh wahh uhh,' before laughing. 'I like that. It provides steady sailing through a stormy sea.'

'Did you learn that exercise when you were in Japan?' I asked.

'Oh yes,' he said. 'From Hoshami. I met him at the International Pretzel Competition in Tokyo. We shared second place. Hoshami could climb trees like a cat. I tried climbing the apple tree once, but I just ended up scaring the rabbits. And myself.'

Priest had read Theodora's journal, and knew everything there was to know about her.

'There are many things to be learnt from Theodora's experiences,' he said. 'She lived alone, yet she managed to build the church and the houses and stay warm in winter. And she read three whole chapters of philosophy every day without fail. She even wrote sermons and tried them out on her goat.'

I looked at the stained glass window. 'Why is she holding a paddle?'

'She canoed down the Thames in a hailstorm,' said Priest. 'She also climbed the highest mountain in Norway. She was a remarkable woman.'

Theodora and her goat were buried in the same grave. No one knew the exact circumstances of how they died, except that they had died together.

Boxman thought that Theodora had attempted a magic trick and that it had gone terribly wrong. But Mama disagreed.

'That woman had no imagination,' she protested. 'Just take a look at her. She was all reason and purpose.'

'But what kind of trick?' I asked.

Boxman looked at me. 'Some tricks are so dangerous, Minou, they are best not spoken about.'

Papa thought that it was impossible to know what had happened to Theodora and her goat and therefore silly to speculate.

But Priest told me in a matter-of-fact voice that Theodora's goat had climbed the stairs to the unfinished church tower, leapt over the edge, and landed on Theodora, who was digging a well right next to the tower.

They were buried at the very same spot when the delivery ship arrived a week later, pulling deep with four hundred and thirty-six bricks for the unfinished wall.

'Did the goat think it could fly?' I asked Priest.

'Perhaps,' he said, 'or maybe it just stumbled.'

Theodora had noticed a change in her goat before the disaster. As she was not one to use big sentimental words, it was noteworthy, said Priest, that in her last journal entry she described her goat as staring out towards sea with a 'peculiar other-worldly longing'.

The boatmen wrote a note on the final page of her diary saying that Theodora still wore her crown when they found her and that they had taken payment for the bricks out of her money tin.

I imagined the goat looking at the world from the church tower; at the ocean, the horizon and maybe the sunrise. I imagined how it might have thought *today is the day* and leapt, waving its little hooves around.

I helped finish the lid to La Luna's box. Boxman had taught me how to paint, and I liked the way it swished when I painted in straight soft strokes. Boxman decide to add gold stars around La Luna's name. His hand moved steadily along the box, frequently dipping the tiny brush in the jar. After a while he stretched, and went to the apothecary's desk to make some honey sandwiches. I sat down with No Name on a bale of hay, scratched his ears and in a whisper told him of the story I was making up about the dead boy, and how I thought that Mama would like it. And No Name looked at me as if he agreed.

'Where is your Papa today, Minou?' said Boxman, placing a plate with two sandwiches next to me. 'I didn't see him cross the forest on his morning walk.

'He is busy,' I said. 'He is looking for the truth.'

'Ah, the truth,' said Boxman and looked at the ceiling. 'I wonder where it is?'

I stared at the ceiling with him. 'He says he is very close to finding the beginning.'

Boxman nodded and took a big bite out of his sandwich. 'That box, Minou,' he said, chewing enthusiastically, 'it reminds me of your mama, she liked the dark blue ones.'

'What else does Mama like?' I asked the question as if it didn't really matter.

'Oh, that's easy,' he said, and smiled in a melancholy kind of way. 'She liked flying carpets. I think she liked them more than anything else in the world.'

I hadn't known that.

I watched Boxman eating his sandwich and wondered why it was that he always seemed to know what Mama liked.

One night during Uncle's visit I overheard Papa and him talking in the kitchen. They talked about Mama. I was drawing in the study and their voices travelled through the house. I could hear glasses being put on the table, and a match being lit, and I could smell Uncle's pipe tobacco.

Papa cleared his throat. 'One morning she liked toast, the next she wanted eggs. And, if there were no eggs, she got sad. It was the same with everything.' Papa cleared his throat. 'Maybe I should get a chicken. Should I get a chicken?'

'Chickens are useful,' said Uncle.

'I never understood what she wanted and why she had to change all the time.'

'Some things are hard to explain,' said Uncle. 'I see that every day in my work.'

'She would say, "We could build a boat, you and I, and sail to the moon and back." And then she would look at me, waiting for me to do something. But what she said wasn't real. We couldn't build a boat just like that.'

Listening in the study I knew straight away what Mama had wanted from Papa. She wanted him to say what Boxman did with ease. 'Let's go then,' he would declare, offering her his arm. 'What will we do on the moon, lovely lady?'

'We will sing,' she would say and smile.

'Well then, let me escort you to the boat. It's here, are you ready?'

It was late when I left Boxman. It was still snowing as I walked along the forest path. We had finished the lid, and I had paint on my fingers and a bit of honey in my hair. Boxman tried to get the honey out, but by rubbing it he made it worse. He ended up declaring that getting messy is the necessary plight of an artist.

I could see our house through the trees in the growing darkness. Smoke rose like a fishbone ladder from our chimney and the windows shone with warmth. Then I noticed the ravens. Undeterred by the falling snow they had settled on our rooftop. Thirty-three of them, sitting in a row. It was strange. The ravens mostly spent their time in the church tower and didn't usually come near our house.

As I reached the front door I realised that I still

hadn't told Boxman about the dead boy. I seemed to keep forgetting. I wasn't quite sure why.

Papa was frying fish at the stove, and the scent of oranges mixed pleasantly with that of fish and onion. 'It's wonderful,' he said, before I had time to close the door behind me, 'when someone listens to you, Minou. There are so few people who care about philosophy.'

'Have you found the beginning yet, Papa?' I pulled off one of my scarves and put it on the table.

'Not quite yet, my girl. It feels as if the boy wants to hear everything I know about Descartes first. There is so much to tell him, Minou. But I have plenty of time. He will be here for another whole day.'

Everything was different the following morning. The house was cold. Papa hadn't lit the fire, and he seemed to have forgotten about breakfast. He had stayed up with the dead boy for the second night in a row, but he no longer looked young and invigorated. He gazed absentmindedly into the coffee pot, and didn't even notice when I put Mama's cup on the table. The coffee boiled over, and he took a long time cleaning it up. After he left for the fishing spot he had to come back twice, first for his bucket, then for his scarf.

I felt sorry for Papa. It didn't seem fair that philosophers had to go through so much trouble searching for the absolute truth. Poor Descartes was summoned by a Swedish queen, who wanted to talk about truth at five in the morning in her very cold castle. And Descartes, who wasn't used to cold castles or getting up early, caught a chill and died.

I got three biscuits out of the jar after Papa had gone, and poured myself a bit of leftover coffee from the pot. I thought that I might have coped better than Descartes with a cold castle and imagined myself, an enormous quill tucked behind my ear, talking to a fair blonde queen who was hanging on my every word.

The blue room had changed overnight. Grainy frost had settled on every surface: on Mama's mural, the cookie tin filled with her flowers and on the dead boy. The lamplight made little snowflake stars on everything it touched. Another raven had joined the first on the sill, and I thought of the many ravens on the roof the night before, and whether they were still there. The snow kept building up inside the window. Papa had moved the chair back next to the dead boy, but I didn't mind. I sat down and pulled the blanket over me.

I noticed a bit of sand on the dead boy's cheek and leaned close to brush it off, but it stuck to his skin. I leaned a little closer and tried to lift one of his eyelids. 'Don't worry, dead boy,' I said. 'It's for Mama. I need to know what colour your eyes are.' But his lids were frozen and it was impossible to move them even the slightest.

I sat back in the chair, opened my notebook, and repeated the title just in case the dead boy had forgotten: 'The curious and interesting story about a boy'. Then I read out loud what I had written the night before in the light of my torch.

The boy's father was a weaver of Persian carpets. One day, a long time ago, one of his carpets flew high up into the air. Everyone was surprised. His father laughed and laughed.

You might think that this house was a fun place to live, but it wasn't. The boy's father only liked weaving at night, and he wanted it to be night all the time. He pulled down the blinds, drew the curtains and lay a doorstopper along the front door. He was not a nice man.

The boy didn't like that it was dark all the time. It was very difficult to read and his torch kept running out of batteries. But the boy's mother didn't mind the dark. She had large hands and loved eating cakes. Every day she would call out, 'I am hungry, hungry, hungry—be quick, be quick,' and every day the boy ran to the baker's shop to buy seven cream cakes.

The streets were loud and bright compared to the house, and the boy tried to see as much as possible on his way there and back. He saw shiny black ravens pecking for crumbs in the snow outside the baker's shop and every day he stopped to pat the butcher's dog that wore a knitted scarf on cold days.

I stopped reading and looked at the dead boy. It looked like he was smiling just a little under the layer of frost. I was proud of the story, it had taken a long time to write. And I especially liked the butcher's dog.

My Mama liked cakes too, and I enjoyed sitting on the wooden bench watching her while she was baking. Sometimes she baked in the morning when it was just getting light, in bare feet and a silk slip. She would pin up her hair with practised movements and open the windows if it wasn't too cold outside.

'We need to breathe, Minou,' she would say.

And I sat on the bench with folded hands and

dangling legs, next to cartons of eggs and her black recipe book.

She made up songs about the island as she lined up the flour, baking powder, orange peel and butter.

'This is a song,' she would sing and smile at me, 'about an island, faaar away, and a girl who caaame to stay.'

'Is the song about you, Mama?' I asked in the brief pause that followed before Mama continued.

'And she had a tiiiny girl, in a tiiiny world.'

Papa would appear, reading glasses on, almost like a cloud of thought in the middle of all the light and air and singing.

'You are baking,' he would inform Mama, looking worried.

'Indeed I am,' she would laugh, flour on her cheek.

Mama's long red hair always escaped the pins. It would sway over cracked eggshells and orange juice, and sooner or later dip into the dough.

Papa said that Mama's hair was like reading Kant: there was always something new and illuminating to be found. But Mama liked it more when Boxman said her hair was like Aladdin's cave. Once he pulled a fishbone from her hair, followed by a green feather. 'You make magic,' he exclaimed, 'without even trying.'

'I could knit you a hairnet,' I said one day when Mama was baking, but she only smiled and kept stirring.

'It's good to do something that makes you feel alive,' she said as she poured batter into a cake tin and handed me the bowl to lick. 'Never forget that, Minou. This cake will come out right, I can feel it.'

Smells stayed on the island. Sometimes I could smell Mama's orange cake under the apple tree, and then again in the corner of Boxman's barn. Priest baked on Sundays, and the scent of his pretzels lingered on the island throughout the week. Once I caught a whiff of them near Theodora's Plateau.

Papa would say with a rare chuckle, 'There is more baking done on this island than philosophical equations.'

But Mama didn't think that it was funny. She didn't like pretzels. 'Salty things,' she said, 'good for nothing.' Every time I left for church she would instruct me, 'Don't bring home any pretzels, Minou, I cannot bear to see any more in your Papa's study.'

But when Priest shook my hand after the

sermon, he would reach into his deep pockets and give me three warm pretzels.

'One for each of you,' he said, sounding so pleased that I couldn't refuse him.

I would take them to Papa, tucked under my jumper where they lay warm against my belly, out of Mama's sight. He would hang them in his study, using the purple ribbons from Mama's chocolate boxes, and admire their shadows at night as they flicked across the books stacked crookedly on the shelves.

When the pretzels began to look a bit old Papa opened the window and threw them towards the forest. 'The rabbits will eat them,' he said. But the rabbits only liked Boxman's cabbages and weren't at all interested in pretzels. I buried the pretzels under the snow every time I found some scattered amongst the trees, worried that Priest would see them.

No Name would come and sit outside when Mama was baking. He would forget to bark at Peacock and just sit there sniffing the lovely smell, waiting with great patience as the kitchen became scattered with orange peel, butter, greased paper and drips of batter.

But the baking always went wrong, even though

Mama did everything right from start to finish. She used twelve oranges as the recipe said, and she whisked the egg whites with sugar until her arm was sore. But the cakes collapsed or didn't taste right, and Mama would cry and say, 'I just want it to be the way it used to be.'

I would sit very still, hoping she would say more about how things used to be, before the island and before she met Papa. But she never did. Instead she would throw large bits of cake to No Name and keep crying.

'See,' she would weep, 'it's only fit for a dog.'

'But No Name has really good taste,' I once protested. And I wanted to tell her that No Name never touched a dead raven and that Boxman said he had a sophisticated palate. But Mama left the kitchen and sobbed behind the bedroom door.

Papa lifted me down from the bench, broke off a piece of cake and tasted it with the look of someone who knew about cakes. Then he gave me a piece and together we would stand in silence, tasting the cake while No Name munched noisily outside.

'It's not bad,' Papa said, 'not bad at all,' and, perhaps because she could hear him, Mama's crying grew louder.

No Name wobbled back through the forest, drunk on cake, and for several days he wouldn't want to play. He just lay, staring into space as if he could see things we couldn't. I thought that maybe he could see where Mama grew up, and all the magnificent cakes that her family used to bake. Maybe he could see what had happened to Mama in the war, before she came to the island, before Papa, with his patient hands, untangled her hair.

There was frost in the dead boy's hair, on his forehead and around his mouth. He looked impatient, and I could almost hear him say, 'More, Minou. Keep reading. It's been a long time since I have heard a good story.'

'Okay, dead boy,' I said. And went on:

Magicians, men of the world, and, of course, Pirate and his Monkey, travelled far to see the carpets. They all hoped to find one that could fly. Cold winds would sweep through the house whenever the boy opened the door. For a moment everything would go bright, but then darkness fell on the corridor once more and the visitors would stumble their way through the house.

The boy made coffee for the visitors. He was the only one who got to see the peacocks, delicately painted in blues and greens on the sides of the coffee cups. Their feathers lit up when he placed them next to the stove.

The boy listened to the conversations of the visitors. He didn't think they noticed him in the darkness. They were mostly busy talking about carpets, but sometimes they would tell stories about the sea. Pirate loved travelling, and had been everywhere. Travelling was his favourite thing. No one, he said, is destined to stay on one island forever. And the boy longed to go with him.

'That's all I have, dead boy. But I will write more later,' I promised.

I wondered if my story might be true. Perhaps the dead boy really had longed to travel, and that's how he ended up on a ship. Was it possible that he, like Uncle, had visited every corner of the world? I thought of Uncle and how he had said that out of the many places he had been, some large, some small, our island was by far the most wonderful.

***

Uncle arrived the morning after the shoe funeral. Papa and I had just gotten up when the boat horn sounded the first time. Dirty plates and glasses still littered the kitchen table from the night before. Papa rolled up his sleeves and began to wash the dishes while I swept. I found five of Priest's paper napkin buffaloes next to the stove where No Name had slept. They were all chewed up, wet and out of shape, and looked more like little balls than buffaloes.

I had watched the funeral from the lighthouse, seeing them all stand in front of the church, dark clothed and stiff from the icy cold. Papa tried to talk me into coming, but I told him that there was no point: Mama wasn't dead.

I could see Boxman weep, while Papa hammered the wooden cross into the hard ground. The cross itself was quite crooked; Boxman had offered to help, but Papa had insisted on doing it himself. He worked on the kitchen table for a whole day and made lots of noise. The first two attempts didn't turn out so well, and we ended up using them to separate the fishing nets when they hung to dry against the wall.

* * *

Uncle had never met Mama, and Papa said it was therefore important that the house looked exactly the way she would have wanted it.

'We need to give your Uncle a good impression,' he said, handing me a bucket with clean soapy water, 'of who your mama was.'

Personally I didn't think Uncle would mind a bit of dust. He had been to every continent, travelled up mountains, down valleys and walked along muddy tracks. He had ridden horses, donkeys and even a cow once, and had definitely seen more than most people. He often sent us long letters about ghost hunting and paranormal phenomena, which is, Papa explained, when you see something that doesn't make sense.

Papa read the letters out loud over dinner. Sometimes he would pause in the middle of an important sentence and say proudly, 'More people should hear about this.' Then he would look at me. 'It is significant research, Minou.'

Mama would make tea while Papa read. One day, while handing Papa a steaming cup, she said, 'I thought you were a man of reason. How can you believe in ghosts?'

'It's a university study,' said Papa. 'They do research.'

Mama shook her head.

'And he teaches,' insisted Papa.

Every letter we received from Uncle started the same way, 'Oh, *mon dieu, mon dieu*, it's been too long!'

'What language is that?' I asked Mama.

'French.'

'Is he French like Descartes?'

'He likes to think he is.'

When Uncle discovered we were related to Descartes he wanted to change his surname. Papa thought it was a wonderful idea, and for days he exclaimed, 'Minou Descartes, Minou Descartes. You can't go wrong with a name like that, my girl.'

But the name change never happened. Uncle couldn't convince anyone that our family tree was genuine. 'The common man,' he wrote to Papa, 'is quick to scoff at perfectly researched fact just because it might be a bit unusual.'

I had almost finished cleaning the floor when the boat horn sounded again, much closer this time.

I handed Papa the bucket, and asked him if Uncle also believed in staying up at night, even though he wasn't a philosopher. But Papa wasn't sure whether Uncle liked late nights. 'You have to remember,' he said, pouring the brown water into the sink, 'that I haven't seen your uncle since the end of the war. However, his letters tell me that he is a man of reason, so it's entirely possible that he likes late nights. He has worked very hard in his field of expertise ever since. I am looking forward to seeing him again and hearing all about it.'

Papa had worked hard too. But, of course, he was searching for Descartes' absolute truth, the start of everything, the key, the explanation of it all.

I didn't hear Papa come back from fishing until he opened the door to the blue room.

'Papa,' I said, surprised, closing my notebook.

'How is he, Minou?' Papa looked grey and tired under his fur hat.

'You have to close the door, Papa. We need to keep him cold.'

'You are right, Minou. You are right.' Papa closed the door behind him. Then he walked slowly to check the temperature on the wall. He looked tired, as if all his energy had escaped him.

He had reached the beach and only caught a

couple of fish before realising that he didn't want to be fishing at all.

'The delivery boat is coming tomorrow morning, my girl. I need to work on the truth while the dead boy is still here. We have got enough fish to get by.' Papa stood back from the thermometer. 'Everything seems fine.' He stifled a yawn. 'I will fix the nets, and make some coffee. Then I will come and sit with him.' And with that Papa left the room.

That was when I found it.

I went to my room to fetch a pair of red woollen socks that Uncle had left behind. The socks were too big for me and too colourful for Papa. The dead boy's bare foot looked very cold under the frost, and I thought that he might like to wear a sock.

One of the ravens was perched on the bedhead when I returned.

'Go away,' I said in a loud voice, shooing it back onto the windowsill, quite certain that the dead boy wouldn't like a raven right next to his head.

It was difficult to put the sock on the dead boy and it took several attempts before I managed to pull it gently over his black toenails and then, bit by bit, ease it on to his icy foot. I got his shoe from the floor. I twisted. I pushed. But getting it on seemed impossible. I turned it around. There was writing on the sole. It said: 'Montgomery's best since 1840' in faded gold lettering. I stopped to copy the words into my notebook and added, 'His shoe smells of oranges too, Mama.'

I put my hand inside the shoe, I am not sure why. But right at the toe was something cold. The ravens looked at me as I brought the shoe to the window and peered into it. I couldn't see anything. But with my hand back inside I felt it again, cold and hard. I edged my fingers around it and pulled and wriggled until it gave way.

It was a metal bottle the size of a small pinecone.

'No wonder you lost your shoe, dead boy,' I said.

The screw-on top was rusty and old, and made a scraping sound when I opened it. Inside was a rolled-up piece of paper. I turned the bottle upside down and shook it hard, but it didn't move. It was only when I used the end of one of Mama's paintbrushes, that I managed to tease it out.

I put the dead boy's shoe back on the floor, and unrolled the paper. It was a postcard. On the front was a picture of a dark-blue ocean and light-blue sky. Distant on the horizon sat a rusty freight ship and out of its chimney came a swirl of stripy smoke.

I felt dizzy. Mama would like it very much. I turned the postcard over. Someone had written on the back. 'What did it say, Minou?' Mama would ask. 'Hurry, hurry, tell me.'

I read the postcard standing next to the dead boy's socked foot. It said:

> I want to tell you this, Levi, although it might not make any sense. It is in the heart and not in the words—not even in the most beautiful ones—but in the heart, in the skeleton bird pushing against your chest, wanting to fly, that we know for certain who and what we love. That is all we have, and all there is.
>
> But right now there is not a cloud in the sky. Right now there is just beauty and light, so much light. Did you get my gift? Yours S

I didn't understand what it meant. Who were Levi and S? The words made me think of the raven skeletons that I had found at the beach, and of the time Peacock died of old age, head resting peacefully on the edge of the golden bowl. Mama had carried him to Priest, who dug a grave right next to Theodora and her goat.

That day I saw Mama cry in Papa's arms. He kissed her, and sang to her in a low humming voice, as she buried her face in his jumper.

'How cold my hands were, how horrible the war was,' she cried. 'Peacock was the only one who knew just how horrible.' And then she sobbed again.

The night before Mama's shoe was to be buried with Peacock I went to the church instead of the lighthouse. Light streamed from the church windows, illuminating the hole in the ground, and I knelt at the slippery edge and drew a picture of Peacock's bones lying deep down in the soil. I thought that Mama would be happy to see what Peacock looked like as a skeleton when she came back.

I turned the postcard over again and attempted to flatten it. Papa would never approve of rolling up a postcard. He was careful with the ones he got from Grandfather, and he got upset if the boatmen accidentally damaged them.

The postcard might not have been addressed to the dead boy, but the name suited him.

'Levi,' I said out loud, and looked at him. 'It's a nice name.'

Then I got up to find Papa. I closed the door carefully behind me and went to the kitchen. But Papa wasn't there. The nets lay in the middle of the floor next to the bucket, and Papa hadn't made coffee or lit the fire.

I found him in the study, asleep on the floor with a pillow under his head. His fur hat was pushed to the side, covering one eye and most of his cheek. I stood uncertain in the doorway with the postcard in my hand. He was sleeping deeply. His shoulder lifted and fell like a wave, and with each breath the pretzels on the ceiling seemed to sway a little.

I looked at the postcards on the wall and then at the box on Papa's desk that was filled with the ashes of Grandfather's work.

When Grandfather was hit by lightning, his housekeeper wrote to us and said the weather had been terrible. But Grandfather, never one to miss his philosopher's walk, had strolled out into a storm so fierce that the lightning looked like stick figures suspended in a crazy dance between earth and sky. His housekeeper even sent us a drawing of Grandfather knocked sideways, his walking stick suspended in the air, as the tree next to him was struck by a gigantic bolt of lightning.

Grandfather must have expected something terrible to happen, because before his walk he took the thousand and seventy-seven pages he had spent thirty years writing and set them alight in the kitchen sink. The curtains caught fire and almost burnt the house down.

None of us went to Grandfather's funeral. It was too far away. But several months later Papa received a box with a note taped to the top saying, 'Your father's life work.' Papa opened the box at the kitchen table, but found only ashes and tiny bits of paper.

'How am I going to find the truth now?' he said, his voice creaking like the rusty gates in the morning. Then he turned to me. 'I promise you, Minou, that when I find the truth, I will share it with you.'

'And with Mama,' I said, looking at Mama who was cutting bread for dinner, her back looking as hard as Turtle's shell.

'And your mama, of course,' he said.

'You should throw it out,' Mama said.

'Maybe,' said Papa, nodding sadly, looking at the ashes. 'There isn't much left.'

'The postcards too, all of it.'

'But Papa needs them,' I said, 'Grandfather knew about the truth.'

Mama gave a sound that was half laugh and half snort.

'He had two philosophical books published,' Papa insisted in a weak voice.

'And who were they published by?' asked Mama, knowing very well that Grandfather had spent all his money publishing them himself.

'Philosophy isn't in fashion,' said Papa.

'I wonder why,' said Mama, throwing the bread into a basket.

'Papa is trying really hard,' I insisted. 'We should help him. He doesn't think he is as smart as Grandfather was.'

'Because I am not.' Papa looked despondent.

'That's not true,' I said. 'You are Descartes' descendant too.'

'Little one.' Mama banged the butter dish on the table. 'Your papa is a lot smarter than that hard-boned, small-minded man.'

'But you never even met Descartes,' I protested.

'I am talking about your grandfather,' she said. 'And your papa should have told you a long time ago that Descartes never had any children.'

She put the dinner plates on the table hard and fast. 'Now we will eat.'

We ate dinner in silence. The ashes of Grandfather's truth still on the table, making everything taste burnt.

That night Papa tucked me into bed.

'How can I be Descartes' descendant,' I asked him, 'if he never had any children?'

'We think he did, Minou, but it's not official,' said Papa. 'You will have to ask Uncle for the specifics. The only thing I know for certain is that we have Danish ancestors. Olga Svendsen is your great-great-great-great grandmother. She lived on the west coast of Denmark where she ran an inn called The Wild Boar. We also know that Descartes travelled past her inn on his way to Sweden.

'But how do you know he stopped at that inn?' I was beginning to feel a bit doubtful about the whole thing.

Papa leant down and gave me a kiss on the forehead, 'Your Uncle works for the university. He is a scholar and an excellent researcher. You can trust him. If he says we are related to Descartes, then we are.'

***

I didn't wake Papa, as he slept deeply on his study floor. Instead I put the postcard in my pocket, feeling the curled-up corners against my fingertips. Then I tiptoed past him and pulled, as quietly as I could, Mama's old atlas from beneath Papa's collection of *Philosophy Today.*

A map of the city hung in the boy's room. Every night he would shine his torch on it and memorise the streets and lanes that led to the harbour.

One morning he reached the baker's shop and kept walking. He didn't stop to get cream buns, and he didn't pause to pat the dog.

He knew exactly where to go. He walked up alleys, down side streets. He hurried past frozen bed sheets hanging on lines, and past shops he had never seen before. He only stopped once when he saw a gold button lying in the snow. He picked it up, put it in his pocket, and rushed on.

The streets near the harbour were busy. There was a hustle and bustle. Men were pulling carts with fish and apples, and the boy almost got run over by a towering barrow of cabbage.

He started to run when he saw the ocean. He ran as fast as he could, and then, as he reached the harbour, he ran straight into a man. He stumbled and would have fallen had the man not caught him.

It was Pirate, with Monkey sitting on his shoulder.

The boy greeted Pirate politely, saying 'How do you do?' while trying not to get too close to Monkey and her sharp teeth.

Pirate and Monkey looked at him for a long time. So long that the boy suddenly got scared that they were going to send him home.

'I believe we have met,' Pirate said.

'I'm not running away,' the boy said and tried to look as if he had business in the harbour and had seen the ocean many times before.

Pirate took his time. He fed Monkey a nut from his pocket with tobacco-stained fingers, looked out at the harbour and said, 'I don't like your father much.'

The boy nodded.

'His house is too dark,' Pirate added. 'I don't trust people who live in dark houses.' He scratched Monkey's ear. 'But I do like his carpets.'

'None of them flies,' said the boy, defiantly.

'I didn't think so.' Pirate sighed and looked regretful. But then he said the magical words, 'Would you like to see my ship?'

My hand was getting sore. It was late afternoon and I had been writing most of the day in the lighthouse.

I put the notebook aside and pulled the postcard from my pocket. I had read it several times during the day, trying to work out what it meant. I was smoothing the edges when the postmark caught my eye. It ran across a faded blue stamp. I could only make out the first two letters, GU. I put the postcard on the mattress and turned to the index of Mama's atlas. There were so many cities beginning with GU. I turned the musty-smelling pages, looking up one after the other, and had almost given up finding anything interesting when I got to the city of Guilin in China. Beneath the map I noticed Mama's handwriting. I pulled the atlas closer and read the tiny letters at the bottom of the page: 'I solemnly swear to visit this magnificent country before I die.'

It was exactly what Grandfather had declared about the great coincidences. Suddenly I remembered what Mama had said to Boxman and me one day when we were practising for the circus.

We had rehearsed almost every day. At lunch we sat on bales of hay in the yard and read Boxman's magazines. One day Mama had found an article about China. It had two pictures. One was of the Sugartop Mountains and the other of a street in Shanghai where hundreds of birdcages hung like lanterns along every shop front. The cages were full of white and yellow birds.

'Look.' Mama showed us the pictures. 'Wouldn't it be wonderful to have a birdcage just like that?'

'And a bird?' I asked and peered at the photo. The bird closest to the camera was a lovely buttery colour. It looked right into the lens with eyes that seemed both kind and intelligent.

'No, little one,' said Mama, 'birds are not for keeping. They should be allowed to fly wherever they want.'

Boxman told us that he had travelled to China once. It had been a magnificent trip and he hadn't wanted to leave. Everything was filled with magic and imagination, he said.

'Are there any suitcases in China?' asked Mama.

'Yes, they sell them on just about every street corner. You should go!'

Mama laughed and said, 'But don't you need a whole year to see all those wonderful things?'

'In fact,' said Boxman, 'a year would be just about right.'

'It's decided then,' said Mama with a big smile. 'I am going.'

I put the atlas down and looked out over the island. The sky was darkening and the snow fell thick and fast, collecting on the pines and burying the forest path. I closed my eyes and thought about Mama's note. The heater rattled, and No Name barked. I thought about it for a long time, and when I finally opened my eyes I knew it to be true, clearly and distinctly. Mama had gone to China. She had gone to the Sugartop Mountains, and then to the street with hundreds of birdcages, and she was showing Turtle all the things we had seen in the magazine.

'How wonderful it would be to stand on one of those mountains with the wind in your hair,' she had said, looking at the pictures, 'or to walk down a street with thousands of birds singing to you.'

* * *

I got my notebook and wrote:

> Truth:
> Mama is in China.
>
> Evidence:
> 1) Mama wrote: 'I solemnly swear to visit this marvellous country before I die.'
> 2) Mama said, 'I am going.'
> 3) Boxman said that to see all of China takes a year.
>
> Deduction:
> Mama will be coming home very soon.

I was contemplating whether I should show Papa the atlas, but decided to wait. Mama would explain it all when she came home. She would sit down at the kitchen table and tell us everything about China. And then she would show me her suitcase, new, blue and shiny like Peacock's tail feathers. 'It reminded me of him,' she would say and point to the blue satin lining inside that matched the exterior leather. Then we would walk to church and dig up her shoe. On the way she would ask me if Priest was still scared of the dark and in the same sentence, before I could answer, she would stretch her arms towards the sky and say, 'Ah it's good to be home, Minou. Your Papa seems changed, like a different person, so full of imagination. The whole island feels changed, so surprising, so interesting.'

I wished that I had come across Mama's note before Uncle came to visit. Then he would surely have listened to me.

Papa and I got to the beach just in time for Uncle's arrival. Remember this was the day after the shoe funeral. The house smelled wonderful and fresh. And at the last minute Papa insisted that I too should get clean. He wanted me to change into something that Mama would have liked, so under my coat I wore a red dress with puffy sleeves. I wasn't pleased. I wanted instead to show Uncle the deep pockets in my green jumper.

The boatmen were unloading our deliveries into the dinghy, as well as a large box of light bulbs for Priest. I was looking for Uncle, suddenly scared he wasn't on board. Priest stepped nervously from side to side, hands stretched in front of him as if to catch the box in case it dropped. We could see the bold red letters in the distance: FRAGILE.

But then Uncle appeared, giving us a feeble wave before gingerly climbing over the railing into the dinghy. He was wearing a bowler hat and a black trench coat. Arriving at the shore he stepped out blindly, one long leg plunging knee deep into the icy water. He walked a few steps and then dropped into the arms of Papa.

Papa had to push him up the hill in the wheelbarrow that Boxman used for carting deliveries. I scrambled after them, carrying Uncle's old and ample suitcase. Uncle's head rested on the handle of the wheelbarrow, his body curled up the way Peacock used to lie in the golden bowl.

'Oh *mon dieu, mon dieu*,' he moaned, just like in his letters, while clutching a black machine tight against his chest.

'Papa, what is that thing?' I called out, while waving at Priest and Boxman, who were still at the beach with their deliveries, waiting for the wheelbarrow to be returned.

'His ghost machine,' said Papa.

'Why is he holding it like that?'

'It makes him feel safe.'

I was eager to speak to Uncle about ghosts and our family tree, and most of all I wanted to show him my notebook and talk to him about Mama. But Uncle slept from the moment we got home, still wearing his trench coat and bowler hat, and woke up only to request one of the chocolates from his bag.

'They are for you,' he said to me, as I looked for them in his big suitcase, 'but I dare not think what will happen if I don't have one now.'

I found the box, fished out a chocolate and gave it to Uncle. He chewed on it and sank back into a deep sleep.

Uncle was eating breakfast the following morning, still in his trench coat and bowler hat. His ghost machine was sitting in the middle of the table surrounded by toast and coffee.

'Pleased to meet you, young lady,' said Uncle, biting into a piece of toast piled high with orange marmalade.

'I was wearing a dress yesterday,' I said, looking at him over the breakfast table.

'You look delightful in that jumper, it goes well with your eyes,' he said.

I looked triumphantly at Papa.

'Have you found any ghosts yet?' I asked, looking at the machine.

'Let's go for a walk before we check,' he said, stretching his legs. 'You can show me the island.' Then he brushed his trench coat free of crumbs and got to his feet, marmalade still stuck to his chin, and with my notebook in hand I went ahead of him out the door. Uncle walked with a stick in one hand and his ghost machine in the other. He walked slowly and bent over, like an injured raven with very long legs. He was puffing on a pipe, leaving a trail of smoke and the scent reminded me of the time Mama burnt a pot of potatoes.

'How old are you?' I asked.

He smiled. 'A bit older than your Papa,' he said. 'The war did us both in.'

As we opened the gates, the wind took his hat and I ran as fast as I could and caught it only moments before it blew into the sea. Walking back to Uncle, I tried to measure his neck for a scarf. He looked pale and cold and I thought a bright red scarf might cheer him up.

'The war steals years from you,' Uncle explained, when I came back with his hat.

'How?' I asked.

'I saw things nobody should ever see.'

'But what, Uncle?' I asked.

Uncle hesitated.

'No one wants to tell me anything about the war.'

'There is one thing. It is not the worst, not by any means or measure, but I keep thinking about it.'

'What is it, Uncle?'

'The war had finished, and I was coming home. Sitting on the train was difficult; I was very thin and tired.'

'Across from me sat a woman, wearing a dress with small violet flowers. She didn't look at me. She was busy eating strawberries from a packet folded out of newspaper. The strawberries were magnificently red. It felt as if I had never seen strawberries that red before. After she finished, even though there was one strawberry left in the packet, she scrunched it up and threw it on the floor. I wanted to eat that last strawberry so much.' Uncle looked out to sea, leaning on his stick. 'I remember everything about that train ride, the woman, the dress, the strawberry. It is the one thing that I can't stop thinking about.'

'The strawberry?'

'Yes, Minou. It follows me everywhere.'

'Like a ghost?

'Yes, sort of like a ghost, but worse.'

'I don't really know what ghosts are,' I said.

'They are complicated creatures like us, Minou, some are good and some bad.'

I thought it strange that Uncle wasn't searching for the truth like Papa. He was after all Descartes' descendant and seemed to be fond of a walk. As we reached the northernmost tip of the island, I asked Uncle why he wasn't a philosopher like Papa and Grandfather.

'I had my own calling, Minou,' he said, 'and your grandfather and I have had quite a few disagreements about it over the years. He was a man purely of reason, not of heart.'

I glanced at Uncle, who slowly and carefully made his way along the beach. Papa was right. He did look both scholarly and trustworthy, although I couldn't be entirely sure, as I had never seen a scholar before.

'How do you know that Descartes had a child with a woman in Denmark?' I asked.

'Rigorous research,' he said.

'But how can you be sure?' I asked.

'There is plenty of evidence, dear Minou. It's all

written in the town hall archives. Olga Svendsen, your great-great-great-great grandmother, had a drawing of Descartes hanging on her bedroom wall. It's safely kept in the town archives today, of course. And I have to say, Minou, Olga was not only a good cook, she was an able artist as well. It only took her a few pencil strokes to capture Descartes' distinct good looks.'

'She might have just liked his philosophy,' I suggested, trying to keep an open mind the way Papa had taught me.

'Yes, Minou. But then there was the menu. She served a fruit-of-the-forest dessert with whipped cream, named *Descartes' Passion*.'

I nodded, pleased to hear that Uncle was good at research. The more he told me about Olga and Descartes, the more certain I was that he would be interested in hearing my argument for Mama still being alive. And I wanted to show him my notebook as soon as possible.

'As a matter of fact,' Uncle continued, 'there was a wealth of information about all sorts of things in the archives. It was remarkable what they wrote down in those days. I even found a section on how to catch eels when you have a cold and need to keep one hand free for blowing your nose.

'I stayed in the town for more than a week. On the last day they held a big party for me with lots of delicacies: herrings, rye bread and cheese, and the room was full of streamers. But I didn't like the food much; I mostly eat toast and marmalade.'

I wondered why no one else knew about Descartes' child, but quickly reasoned that if Descartes had died not long after arriving in Sweden, then Olga might not have had a chance to tell him that she was pregnant. Or maybe Descartes hadn't given her the address of the castle. But, if he hadn't given Olga the address, then maybe he was an awful person like Rousseau, who, Mama told me, went out into the world to serve the Enlightenment, leaving behind his wife and five children.

'What does the Enlightenment mean?' I asked Papa.

'It means,' said Papa, 'that Rousseau wanted the best for everyone. He wanted a new world where people were happy and free.'

I imagined five hungry children standing on a cold floor, waiting for their father to come home and enlighten them as well. Later I dreamed that they came to visit me, freezing and shivering. In my dream I knitted five long scarves, one for each of them, and when I woke in the morning I had unravelled a whole ball of wool.

Walking next to Uncle, I wondered if I could trust Descartes' way of finding the truth if he had been an awful man. But then I reminded myself that logic could be held up against bad weather, and years without apples on the apple tree, and had nothing to do with either kindness or love.

No Name barked again. I could see him, tiny in the distance, running across the beach. The ocean was churning grey with snow and broken ice.

My stomach rumbled. It was almost dinnertime, but it was quiet downstairs and I thought Papa was still asleep.

No Name reached the forest and was running very fast. I thought he might be chasing a rabbit. When I was little I used to worry about the rabbits when it got cold. I couldn't imagine how they kept warm in winter. But Papa had assured me that they had burrows to hide in and could easily dig their way through all the snow.

The rabbits were shy. No Name had never caught any and I had only ever managed to catch one. It happened when I was six, and Papa still remembered it as one of the worst days of his life, worse even than the cellar, he said.

I brought a small sturdy box to the forest. It had previously contained twelve jars of paint that Mama had ordered from Belgium, and it had a lid with a shiny silver latch. I set it on its side near the apple tree and placed a whole cabbage inside it. Then I waited for a long time. By noon my stomach started rumbling and I was contemplating running home for a sandwich, when, at last, a lovely little rabbit jumped into the box and started nibbling the cabbage. I quickly closed the lid, secured the latch and lifted the box. It was very heavy. I had to put it down several times before I reached the beach and when I finally put it into Mama's rowboat my arms felt fluttery and much longer than usual.

The tide was high, and even though I was little, I managed to push the rowboat into the sea. I climbed aboard and sat next to the oars as I had done on land so many times before, pretending that I was Mama, arriving at the island, waving to Papa on the shore.

The ocean took the boat and pulled it out to sea. It felt wonderful. I opened the lid to the box and the rabbit stuck its head out and looked at the water. I sat next to him like Mama had sat next to Peacock.

I didn't really notice how fast we were drifting out to sea, but suddenly I was far from shore.

It was then that I saw Papa on the beach. He was calling out, 'Minou, Minou, what are you doing, what are you doing, my girl?' I waved to him, and wondered if I was just as colourful as Mama had been when she arrived. I was wearing a green dress and my dark blue scarf. I had just learnt to knit and the scarf had several holes in it, but I thought the colours went well together. And I wondered if Papa could see the rabbit. I got it out of the box and held it up for him. But when I got to my feet, the boat tipped and I almost fell out. Now I could no longer see Papa, but I could hear Mama calling, and saw her running down the path to the beach. And then I saw Papa in the water. He was swimming towards me, calling out, 'Sit down, Minou, sit down.'

Papa had never taught me to swim, he said the ocean was far too dangerous for us to practise in, and I could see that he was struggling in the waves. All at once being in the boat didn't feel so good. The rabbit gave these tiny wheezing sighs, and looked at me with stiff eyes. When Papa reached the boat he was puffed and his hair was wild. Mama stood on the beach and waved. But she didn't look happy. And when Papa rowed us back, she got me by the arm and pulled me up the path, shouting and crying, and I wasn't allowed to go out for three days. Papa released the rabbit on the beach, but it was so scared that it stayed on the same spot until nightfall.

It was getting darker. I looked up from the notebook and noticed it had stopped snowing. No Name was nowhere to be seen. Boxman's yard was empty but the barn door was open, and I was sure he had gone back inside. I thought of how Uncle and I had walked through the forest on our way to visit Boxman. We had seen several grey rabbits darting across the path, and I told Uncle the story of the rabbit and the boat. Uncle laughed, then stopped in front of the apple tree, admiring its bare branches, shaking his head.

'Three hundred and two apples, you say.'

'Boxman had a stomach ache for a week.'

When we arrived Boxman was sitting on a bale of hay in the middle of the yard playing his accordion. He was wearing his blue cape, and played with gusto, swinging here and there, even though he had once told me that musicians need to be careful not to get carried away.

'There is only so far you can follow a tune before it starts to get dangerous,' he said.

One night Boxman played a particularly sorrowful tune in his yard. It built up, getting faster and faster, wilder and wilder, like a horse galloping out of control. Then, with a horrible screech, he stretched the accordion so far that he dislocated his shoulder, dropped his cigarette in fright and burned a hole in the instrument. And Papa, who was sleeping, yelled, 'Let me out. Let me out.'

'Sometimes,' explained Boxman, 'sadness has a sweet, enchanting edge. It pulls at your heart and you can't get enough.'

'What were you sad about?' I asked.

'I kept seeing Cosmina in the Himalayas gazing at the stars, her hands all cold. And I thought, what if she wants to find me and doesn't know the way?'

Boxman put the accordion down and stood up when he saw us. He shook Uncle's hand, and inquired straight away about the ghost machine.

'I am a researcher of paranormal phenomena,' said Uncle.

'Is that a dangerous profession?' asked Boxman.

Uncle shook his head. 'Only when you research at night and risk tripping over things.'

No Name didn't take any notice of Uncle. He was too busy barking at the tins of dog food piled high on Boxman's wheelbarrow. Every tin had 'Happy Dog' on the label and sported a black terrier with a pearly white smile.

'I noticed the tins on the ship,' said Uncle, as we followed Boxman into the barn. 'But I had no idea they were for such a delightful dog. He looks like a frisky encounter with life itself.'

And all of a sudden I saw Boxman and No Name the way Uncle might see them. They looked almost as mysterious as The Great Shine and his tiger. And the barn felt different too. It looked the way it did the first time we visited Boxman after his arrival on the island.

For weeks the boatmen had delivered his things. They had to go back and forth in the dinghy so many times that I lost count, and they were tired and grumpy by the end of it. I was eager to pay Boxman a visit. But Mama said that it wasn't polite to drop in on someone uninvited, and that he was most likely busy putting away all those interesting things he had brought to the island. I got terribly impatient.

But just as I felt I couldn't wait any longer, Boxman appeared at our door and asked us to come for punch that night.

Mama wore her prettiest dress. It was blue with a tight belt around her waist, and she wore a dark red rose in her hair. She wasn't shy like the rest of us, but walked around the barn, examining everything, opening drawers and turning things over.

Papa, Priest and I stood in the middle of the room, each holding a glass of red punch, which Boxman assured us only contained sparkly raspberry juice and finely sliced pineapple.

Papa asked Boxman if he had been in the war.

Boxman shook his head as he refilled Priest's glass. 'I was young when it broke out,' he answered. 'I was working on a ship with my father. He was a magician too. We stayed abroad until it had all finished.'

Later, Priest inspected the box on Boxman's worktable. Painted on the side was a man with a deer's head and the words: 'Transformation or transfiguration, you choose!'

Priest looked at the box with awe. 'My dear Boxman, you must tell us how this works,' he said.

Boxman asked us if we wanted to try and lie in

it, but Papa said that it reminded him too much of the root cellar, and Priest was scared of the dark. Mama was investigating the apothecary's desk at the other end of the barn, and I was too shy to say yes.

Boxman had just started explaining the box trick, when Mama yelled, 'Oh, look,' so loud that it made us all jump. She had found a parcel wrapped in purple paper. It had a little card, decorated with a bird in flight, attached to it. The card said: 'For the Madame of the island.'

'Is that for me?' she asked.

Boxman feigned surprise. 'What in the whole wide world could that be?'

Mama unwrapped it quickly and unveiled a pair of turquoise silk gloves. 'They are beautiful,' she exclaimed and held them up so Papa could inspect them. She gave Boxman a kiss on the cheek. 'Thank you,' she said. 'They are exquisite.'

'I have something for you too,' Boxman said to me. 'But I am afraid I might have forgotten where I put it.' He winked at me.

Everyone tried to help me.

'Warm,' said Boxman, as I walked along the wall of boxes, 'warmer, cold, freezing, a little bit warm.'

'Go to the left, Minou,' shouted Mama.

'No, maybe in the corner,' suggested Priest.

'Yes, try the corner, Minou, next to the apothecary's desk,' said Papa, and they were all laughing.

I found the present under Boxman's bed. It was a pair of knitting needles adorned with small lion heads. 'There seem to be a lot of scarves on this island,' he said, looking at Papa and Priest and myself in turn. 'I thought that it might just be possible that you were the creator.'

I decided that I would start a scarf for Boxman that night.

Boxman gave Papa a paperweight, and Priest, who had pretzels in the oven, left early with a clock in his pocket. He didn't get to see when Boxman made Mama's gloves vanish behind a silk scarf, only to have them reappear in Papa's pocket.

'What a wonderful exciting thing to have happen to us,' said Mama, and put her arm in Papa's as we were walking home. Her cheeks were glowing.

Papa took my hand. 'I wonder if Boxman has read T.S. Somer,' he said. 'He is a little known philosopher, but he writes extensively about the metaphysical impossibility of disappearance.'

Mama said, 'Well, my love, it looks to me like Boxman is managing to make things vanish just fine. And how refreshing it is to see a man with such passion.'

Standing next to Uncle I saw Boxman's barn the way I had all those years ago. Boxman explained once again how the magic box trick worked, and when Uncle admired the apothecary's desk, he was invited to open any drawer he liked. Uncle was excited. He placed his ghost machine and walking stick on top of the desk and began to open one drawer after the other. In the first drawer was a measuring tape. In the second a globe. In the third a punnet of gooseberries, and in the fourth an enormous snake that I had never seen before. Uncle jumped back and, without his stick, almost lost his balance. I helped him sit down on a bale of hay, while the snake swayed life-like in Boxman's hands.

'It's made from nineteen melted bike tyres,' Boxman gazed proudly at the snake. 'It's a copy of Sigurd.'

Uncle and I must have looked puzzled.

'Sigurd was the greatest dancing snake in history,' Boxman explained. 'Some say he is still alive.'

'Was he dangerous?' I asked, looking at the dark glinting eyes of the snake. 'Sigurd,' said Boxman, giving the snake an affectionate pat, 'killed ninety people. The last to die was the snake charmer himself.'

'That's too sad,' I said, as I passed Uncle his ghost machine.

'Especially,' said Boxman, 'because it is well known that the charmer was fond of Sigurd. He had never before owned a snake that could dance to all kinds of music, whether it was tango, blues or jazz. His last words were, "Keep dancing, Sigurd."'

After the snake charmer collapsed, the snake retreated into the basket. The market square was abandoned in seconds, even though it was the middle of the day and the busiest time for buying gulab jamun, sweet fried balls in rose syrup.

The basket, Boxman told us, sat in the empty square, first in the sun, then in the shade, before evening arrived. From his window, an old man who liked night better than day saw someone walk across the square, humming a tune. The person, it was impossible to tell whether it was a man or a woman, went straight to the basket and, still humming, picked it up and walked away.

But no one believed the old man. He was not always on his best behaviour. He stole from the stall holders at the market, sometimes socks, sometimes apples and once a watermelon hidden under his shirt, and every morning with impeccable timing, he flashed on the street corner, amusing anyone who was around to notice.

For years everyone thought that Sigurd was still somewhere in the town. They looked under their beds at night and, as most people in the town had big feet, they also made sure to check their shoes each morning.

Uncle looked faint during this story.

'What an adventure,' he said breathlessly when Boxman finished, and then he gave a strange laugh that ended in a swallow. 'I don't know why,' he continued, 'but that snake, Minou, reminds me of the woman with the strawberries.'

I went over and sat next to him. 'The snake isn't real,' I said, patting his hand. It was freezing cold. 'You have to think logically when you get scared,' I continued. 'Logic is all we've got, says Papa. It's a shield against snowstorms and other scary things.'

Uncle nodded, still looking pale, and then told me that he used to be scared of ghosts.

'Aren't you scared anymore?' I asked.

'I starting looking straight at them,' he said. 'Then they stopped coming so close.'

I thought about this. 'Do you want me to get the snake, Uncle, so you can look straight at it?'

Uncle shook his head. 'I don't think I am quite up to it, dear Minou.'

'Cosmina didn't like the snake either,' said Boxman. 'She said it reminded her of Russia.'

'Cosmina is Boxman's great love,' I explained to Uncle. 'She has red hair like Mama.'

'And where is the charming young lady?' asked Uncle.

'She is gazing at stars in the Himalayas,' said Boxman. 'She doesn't need to be rescued anymore.'

'She sounds like a wonderful young woman,' replied Uncle. 'Full of initiative.'

Uncle kept looking nervously towards the apothecary's desk even after Boxman had put the snake back in the drawer. He didn't relax until we left the barn and were on our way to the church.

Priest was excited to have visitors. After greeting us, he left us waiting on the doorstep so he could get changed into the violet robe he wore on special occasions or when he needed a bit of cheering up.

I wanted to talk with Uncle about Mama, but when Priest returned in his violet robe he began to tell Uncle all about Theodora and the frescoes. When

Uncle saw the stained glass window he exclaimed that Theodora looked distinctly like Descartes' father.

'He had the same determined look in his eyes,' he said. 'I wonder if there is a connection. Wouldn't that be brilliant, Minou, if there was?'

I told him that No Name was scared of the black dog in the row of angels.

'I am too,' said Uncle. 'Look at those teeth.'

Priest and Uncle talked for a long time and Uncle ate three large pretzels. But finally Uncle shook Priest's hand and asked me to show him Mama's shoe grave.

This was my chance.

'She is not there,' I said. 'It's only her shoe. And Peacock of course.'

Then I proceeded to tell Uncle, step by step, as logically as I could, my argument for Mama still being alive. When we got close to her shoe grave, I showed him my notebook and told him that there was no reason to pay attention to a shoe that Mama could have lost in any number of ways. I also showed him my sketch of Peacock's skeleton. Uncle looked at the sketch and listened to all I had to say.

Encouraged, I told him about the sunken city

and of the octopus that had jumped straight from the scales. And I told him about the man from one of Boxman's magazines, who was eaten by a boa constrictor and rescued by one long cut of a Swiss army knife, just when he could hold his breath no longer. There was a picture of him throwing an omelette into the air like a professional chef. His cat was in the photo, too, sitting on the kitchen bench, looking sceptically at the midair omelette.

I reminded Uncle that Descartes would have closed his eyes and said, 'Let me think about it for a bit longer. It is only my thoughts that count, not a shoe.'

And as I spoke it felt like Mama was about to arrive home at any moment.

When we reached the grave Uncle asked, with a kind but sad expression in his eyes, 'Where would she have gone, Minou?'

And I couldn't answer.

Then he took off his bowler hat, bowed his head, and looked mournful. And it was clear that Uncle wasn't going to help me convince anyone that Mama was alive.

How surprised they would all be when she walked in the door and wanted her shoe back. She would laugh and say, 'But I am not dead, how silly.'

Mama would know straight away what the dead boy's postcard meant. She would say, in a matter-of-fact voice, 'Yes, Minou, I too have a skeleton bird inside of me. Everyone does.' And she would tell me how a freight ship had picked her up the day she left the house with Turtle and her large black umbrella. 'Can you believe it?' she would say. 'They were going to China too.'

She would laugh again and describe the ship in great detail, from the enormous chimney billowing black smoke, to the load of colourful silk blankets stacked from floor to ceiling on the lowest deck where she shared a cabin with a snake charmer. She would tell me how she had slept with one eye open, watching the snake basket. The snake wanted to dance every time it heard the foghorn, so it was most important for her to stay alert.

I put the postcard back in my pocket, and placed the atlas next to my orange scarf. I was hungry. The delivery boat was coming in the morning and I needed to wake Papa if he hadn't already started dinner.

Papa had kept up Mama's tradition after she disappeared. She used to cook for everybody on the island the night before the delivery boat came. One joy should never arrive alone, she said, as she sent me off down the forest path, delivering bowls of steaming food to Priest and Boxman. Mama liked to experiment, and Boxman used to say that her cooking marked the most interesting day of the week. But he didn't always like the food, and a few times Mama's chocolate fish fillets ended up in No Name's bowl.

Papa, on the other hand, could only make two dishes and, even though we all liked fried fish and pancakes, it wasn't as exciting as it used to be.

I left the lighthouse. It was getting very cold outside and my breath turned to mist as I walked down the stairs. But it was just as cold in the kitchen. The fire still hadn't been lit and Papa wasn't cooking dinner. I could hear him in the blue room, talking softly, but there was something about his voice that didn't sound right. I tiptoed close and listened at the door.

'Dear boy,' I heard him say, 'I can't work it out. Is the beginning in your gold button, or in your foot? Or is it somewhere else?' Papa seemed to swallow a sob. 'Oh, dear boy, I wish you could tell me.'

Suddenly I felt hungry and terribly cold. The orange smell seemed far too sweet, and I missed Mama. I missed the way she used to be busy at the stove, her red hair tied up, her pale face flushed from the heat. I missed the way her dress used to move, back and forth, like music, as she cooked for us.

I got the last biscuit out of the jar, and tried to imagine what Mama might have done to make everything feel better. And I remembered the French song she sang at the circus.

I went and stood in the middle of the kitchen, cleared my throat, and began to sing. The words were in French and I didn't understand what they meant, but I thought that I pronounced them right. I had listened to Mama sing it many times during our rehearsals.

By the third verse the room started to feel nicer. I could almost hear Mama say, 'See, Minou, bring a little joy into the house and everything feels different. It's like magic.' And it was true, even the apples that she had painted next to the shoe rack seemed brighter.

Mama's song was only a small part of the circus. We had been practising our tricks for weeks and when the night of the performance arrived I was sitting on the bed, watching Mama put up her hair. She was wearing an olive dress that looked beautiful against her hair. Her red suitcase sat next to me, packed and ready, filled with costumes. The old cookie tin was open and Mama's flowers were spread out on the dressing table. There was a red, white, yellow, green and a pale blue one.

'This would look beautiful against your black hair.' Mama held up the pale blue flower.

I shook my head, 'I don't like things in my hair, Mama.' I crossed my legs on the bed and looked at the suitcase. 'It's as if we are going to the other side of the world,' I said, tracing the locks on the suitcase, thinking they looked like No Name's ears when he went flying through the burning hoop in the yard at night.

She smiled. 'The other side of the world is far away.'

'Boxman has a second heart,' I said.

'A second heart?' Mama decided on a white flower shaped like a lily.

'On his chest.'

'Not an apple?'

'No,' I said bewildered.

'Not a pear?' Mama was smiling. 'Or a suitcase?' She fastened the flower behind her ear.

'No, don't be silly Mama.'

She looked at her reflection in the mirror. 'To have a second heart would be a wonderful thing. You could receive visitors at any time, with no notice at all.'

'You don't have visitors in your heart,' I protested.

'Oh, but you do,' she insisted, a hairpin between her teeth, 'and if you had a second heart you could say, "Come in, my heart is nice and pure."'

I didn't think she made much sense.

'Like yours, little one, or mine, when I was younger...'

'What was it like when you were younger, Mama?'

But Mama was already putting on her shoes and didn't seem to hear my question. 'We should leave, Minou. Boxman has been working in the barn all day, he needs our help.'

The rain had been falling silently, and the path was wet and slippery. We walked through the dark forest, dragging the red suitcase between us. Mama lifted up her dress to avoid the puddles, and she laughed when we almost slipped and had to cling to each other to keep our balance.

'Little one,' she said, 'this is going to be a night we will never forget, I can feel it.'

Just before we reached Boxman's yard we saw lights, hundreds of them, running along the barn, reflected in the wet courtyard.

'It all looks so magical,' exclaimed Mama as we entered the barn.

The stage was fringed with pine branches and a great big mirror was leaning against the back wall for costume changes. A heavy velvety curtain in a brilliant green hung at the side of the barn, ready to be pulled across the stage. Candles were lit everywhere, some alarmingly close to the hay bales. But

Boxman had assured me that nothing would catch fire and that he would place a bucket of water in each corner just in case.

There were six rows of chairs with different coloured cushions, and streamers that stretched from one end of the barn to the other. Boxman wore a slim pinstriped suit with green socks and pointy shoes, and his hair was brushed and hanging loose. He bowed gallantly, kissed Mama's hand and then mine.

'You are not wearing a cape today,' I said.

'No,' he answered, 'today is special.'

Mama sent me behind the curtain to get changed. I stood, shivering in my underwear, while she looked for my clown jacket in the suitcase. No Name, who was wearing his new brown cardigan, came up to say hello. The cardigan was the first I had ever made. It was a bit tight around his belly, stretching the buttonholes, but I thought I had done a good job and No Name looked pleased with it.

It was only when I had put on the clown jacket and Mama had painted my cheeks red that I realised I had left my clown shoes at home. Boxman said not to worry. He went to the apothecary's desk and pulled a pair of huge white shoes from a tiny drawer.

'These were worn by Bukowski, the great Hungarian clown,' he said. 'He wore them at his infamous performance in Warsaw.'

'Why was it infamous?' I asked.

'He had a new-found passion for tightrope walking and didn't care about falling anymore. He cared for falling in love. That night he walked the tightrope dressed in pink, matching his trapeze girlfriend, Frida the Quick. He didn't fall once and the people of Warsaw never forgave him.'

I tied the laces twice around my ankles to keep them on, but was still about to walk out of the huge white shoes every time I took a step. I went up and down the rows of chairs practising, while Mama did singing exercises in the corner and Boxman stood on a ladder trying to attach a bright stage light to a wooden beam.

'Why do we need so many chairs?' I asked.

'You should always expect more people,' said Boxman from the ladder. '"Expect surprises," my old ringmaster used to say, "it will keep you on your toes."'

It was almost as if we were in a real circus and people were queuing up outside, and elephants were waiting to perform, snorting and rocking the way Boxman said they did just before going on stage.

Mama stopped her singing exercises. 'I shouldn't be doing this,' she said to Boxman. 'This is a circus not a theatre. Who wants to hear me sing?'

'I do,' I said.

But Mama ignored me. 'I should have just assisted you,' she said to Boxman. 'Why did I want to do something on my own? What a stupid idea.'

But Boxman assured her that her singing would make it a circus like no other and that it was normal to be nervous. 'Take some deep breaths,' he said.

Mama was assisting Boxman in his box trick. She was also supposed to help him with No Name's fire jumping, but had changed her mind. She didn't want to let me help either, even though it was difficult for Boxman to yell and hold the hoop at the same time.

Mama used to hold No Name's hoops while Boxman was yelling, but it all went wrong when Boxman added fire to the hoops. No Name didn't like it much. And during a rehearsal a few weeks before the performance he ran away howling and hid in the barn.

'This is cruel,' said Mama in a shrill voice and threw the burning hoop on the ground. It hissed in the snow, leaving dark petrol-coloured marks.

Boxman stood still. Only his cape moved in the wind. Then he waved his finger at Mama. 'You think you know about animals,' he said. 'But you don't. Because of you No Name will think he is a failure.'

Mama didn't listen. She walked up to Boxman, swiftly took his finger in her mouth and bit him hard. Boxman said nothing, even though it must have hurt. He turned and followed No Name into the barn, his footsteps dumb in the snow.

'Come,' said Mama, pulling me off the bale of hay, where I had been audience to No Name's rehearsal. She walked briskly ahead, pulling me down the forest path. Her dress took on a life of its own, brushing over Boxman's cabbages, pale and green, sticking out of the snow.

I didn't understand Mama's smile when she undressed in our kitchen, stripping down to her silk underwear. Her white legs were luminous as she turned in front of the fire.

'It's cold,' she said to Papa, when he came in and saw her standing there. Then she laughed. And Papa and I, we couldn't help it, we laughed too.

* * *

But that was the lead-up. The hour had arrived.

'I am still nervous,' Mama said, after she had been breathing deeply for a while.

'Don't be nervous, you are magnificent,' said Boxman from the ladder. 'And you look wonderful with the flower in your hair.'

'Okay,' she said, 'okay.' She took another breath, walked to the middle of the stage and, with the voice of a ringmaster exclaimed, 'Ladies and gentlemen, this is going to be an extraordinary performance.'

'Yes!' shouted Boxman, wobbling dangerously on the ladder.

'People will talk about it for years to come. How the magnificent three—'

'Four,' I interrupted, pointing to No Name who was sniffing the pine branches.

'Four,' repeated Mama. 'People will ask far into the future, "Where are they now? What are they doing?" And people will say, "Remember that little girl with the raven hair and the big white shoes?" Everyone will—'

'But Mama,' I interrupted again, 'it's only Papa and Priest.'

She nodded, 'That's true, but—'

'And where is Papa going to sit?' I asked.

Mama stopped being a ringmaster and said in her normal voice, 'There is plenty of space, Minou; six rows of chairs.'

'Yes,' I said, 'but he doesn't like to choose.'

Papa arrived, damp but handsome in his suit and bowtie. He smiled and waved, but stopped when he saw the rows of chairs.

I ran towards him as fast as I could in Bukowski's shoes, searching for a good seat. I saw one that looked nice, right in the middle of the second row with a gold pillow on it. I went and took his hand. 'This one is for you, Papa,' I said.

'Thank you, my girl. Thank you,' he said again, accidentally stepping on my big shoes.

Priest arrived, wearing his violet robe, holding an umbrella and a bouquet of tulips in one hand and a plate of pretzels in the other. He glided onto the chair next to Papa, and I could hear him tell Papa how he had seen all the lights in Boxman's yard from the church tower as he got changed into his robe.

'A guiding light,' he exclaimed. 'Such a welcome.'

A silence fell over the barn. Boxman folded up the ladder, put on his top hat and went to the centre of the stage. He started out in a quiet voice, 'Ladies and gentlemen,' then he got louder, 'you are about to see,' then bellowed, 'a singer of great renown.' He pronounced 'renown' as if the word tasted sweet.

Priest whispered to Papa, 'A singer? How unexpected. Who could it be?'

Boxman bowed, doing a round wave with his hand, almost as if he were making the shape of a fire hoop. Papa and Priest clapped and Boxman nodded for me to pull the curtain string. And there was Mama, standing with an old microphone between her hands.

She looked beautiful, like a seahorse, like the ones we saw coming close to shore, standing upright, but floating at the same time.

Boxman put the accordion to his chest. And Mama sang as if she were somewhere else, as if Boxman's barn was full of things none of us had seen before. She sang in French. Her voice was like Boxman's sharp-edged saw, like the ocean on a windy night. It seeped sorrowfully through the hay bales, the barn and the rain outside. Boxman cried, tapping his foot to the rhythm while his tears fell into the accordion. Papa and Priest seemed mesmerised, and No Name followed Mama's movements intently from his spot near the stage.

'I didn't know your mama could speak French,' Papa said in the short break that followed. And when Mama came out from behind the curtain and waved me backstage, he smiled at her almost shyly, as though they hadn't met before.

No Name had to get out of his cardigan before he could perform in the burning hoop trick. The barn smelled of petrol and Boxman yelled in an angry voice, 'Come, come, come, jump...yes... Hoopla!' And No Name didn't look nervous at all. He jumped through the hoop twice, and seemed to like the applause. Even Mama clapped.

Then it was my turn.

'Clowns fall,' Boxman had explained during practice.

'But won't everyone feel sad when I fall?' I asked.

'Yes, but if you do it well, then they will also laugh,' he answered. 'You will make them feel happy and sad. That's the art of being a clown. But it's important that you remember to pause between your falls. Otherwise the audience will get worn out by all that emotion.'

During my act, I remembered to pause. I fell over imaginary things, waited, then fell again, while Boxman played a dramatic tune on the accordion.

'Imagine that there is something in front of you,' Boxman had said during practice. 'Elephants, hats, bottles with thick green bubbling liquid, a cloud, another clown, an old key, imagine it all and fall.'

At my first fall Priest gave a frightful cry. Papa tried to assure him that I was fine. 'She is a clown,' I heard him say, 'she is supposed to fall. She is doing a wonderful job.'

But at my next fall Priest shouted, 'Watch out, Minou, watch out.'

He startled Boxman, who for a moment stopped playing, and when I took my final bow I saw that Priest was clutching Papa's hand, making it hard for either of them to clap.

It didn't get better during the box trick. Mama was a good actress. She trembled as she crawled into the box and Priest clung to Papa during the entire act.

I had seen Mama and Boxman rehearse it many times, and I didn't like to watch when Boxman raised the saw and Mama started to moan, 'Oh no, no, no. Don't saw me in half. Please Mister, please. Spare me. There are many other women out there, why me? I like my legs.' Boxman acted as if he didn't hear her and the saw went grate, grate, grate through the wood.

Papa and Priest couldn't stop clapping when Mama emerged unharmed from the box. She bowed several times and sent them lots of kisses. Then she nodded for me to draw the curtain. The applause died down and the barn fell quiet. Boxman climbed the ladder and readjusted the spotlight so it shone a soft pink. Then he joined Mama behind the curtain.

The rain tapped softly on the roof, and the barn smelled of candle wax. No Name sat alert on a chair next to Priest.

I was standing at the side of the stage, waiting for Mama's cue. And when she whispered, 'We are ready, Minou,' I pulled the curtain.

Boxman was wearing his top hat, and Mama a dress that shimmered and sparkled like gold. They both stood still, gazing straight ahead, and looked just like one of Mama's paintings. Over a stool next to them lay a large piece of red silk. Then Boxman moved. He approached the stool, picked up the silk and went back to Mama. I walked across the stage and removed the stool. Everyone was quiet. Bukowski's shoes clicked loud against the floor.

Boxman held the bundle of silk. He looked at Mama, who nodded, and then he lifted his arms in a rapid movement. The silk unfurled in front of Mama, hiding her. Then, just as quickly, he pulled the silk back.

Mama was gone.

Papa leaned forward in his chair, and Priest stood up so abruptly that No Name growled.

Boxman took a deep breath, and then, with the same swift arm movement, he flashed the silk again. It billowed in the air, and when it fell, Mama was standing in the very same spot she had been before.

Papa and Priest roared. They cheered, they clapped and when Mama, Boxman and I held hands and bowed, Papa stamped his feet on the ground making a great wall of noise. Afterwards he told me that it is a tradition to stamp your feet if you enjoy a performance.

Priest was flushed. 'What a miracle,' he said. 'What an astonishing thing to have been sawn in half and vanish, yet still,' he threw out his arms in exclamation, 'be so beautiful.'

Then he remembered the tulips and threw them at Mama, hitting her on the arm.

'But where did you get these, dear Priest?' She laughed and wasn't mad at all. 'And in the middle of winter.'

Priest beamed and looked pleased with himself, 'Oh I have my ways, I have my ways,' he said.

Papa appeared in the kitchen, white-faced under the fur hat, as I finished Mama's song.

'But what are you doing, Minou?'

'I am making everything feel better, Papa.'

Papa noticed the cold fireplace and the night sky.

'I am sorry, my girl,' he said, and went straight to the kitchen bench, getting out fish, potatoes and an old cabbage. Then he walked into the yard, leaving the door open, and soon after I heard the sound of his axe.

Snow had built up along the doorstep, and Papa almost slipped over when he returned with his arms full of firewood. He knelt in front of the fireplace and arranged the kindling, then the bigger logs. When the flames began to wheeze and crackle, Papa got to his feet and brushed his pants. He stared sorrowfully at the tiny blaze. It seemed as if he had forgotten that I was there. The fire flickered, and Papa said, 'I can't find the truth. Your mama would be so disappointed in me.'

'Mama doesn't like the truth,' I said in a firm voice. 'She likes blue boxes and flying carpets.'

Papa looked confused. 'Flying carpets? Are you sure, Minou? She never mentioned anything about flying carpets.'

'Boxman says that flying carpets are her most favourite thing in the whole world, Papa. He knows a lot about Mama.'

'Right,' said Papa and cleared his throat. Then he bent down to push a piece of wood closer to the fire. With his back to me, he said, 'You better get dressed, Minou. Dinner will be ready soon.' He glanced out the window. 'The snow is deep. You will have to walk carefully.'

I set out for the church with the notebook tucked under my arm and a steaming plate of fish in each hand. Snow crunched under my feet and the moon had appeared over the water, low and full, even though night was still to fall.

Priest opened the church door wearing his violet robe and two of the scarves I had knitted him. He looked feverishly pale, but greeted me cheerfully. 'So lovely of you to come,' he said and sniffled. 'And you have brought fish, I see. Come in, come in.'

Two picnic blankets were spread next to the altar with cheeses, wine, candles and a pile of origami paper.

'Sit down, dear Minou,' he said, gesturing towards the blanket.

'Are you sick, Priest?' I sat down and put my notebook and the plates on the picnic blanket.

'I am a bit under the weather, but,' he looked affectionately at the cross, 'we were just having fun, God and I. There is never a dull moment, Minou, when you are with God.' He blew his nose in a large handkerchief.

'What happens if you spill on your robe?' I asked.

'God will make sure that doesn't happen.'

But later when Priest spilled wine right down the front of his robe, he exclaimed contentedly, 'God is reminding me of an exquisite spread.'

Priest pointed at the cheeses and told me their names. There were camembert, brie, blue vein and then one that smelled very bad.

'It is called The Old Cheese,' said Priest, and smiled at my expression. 'Yes, I was frightened too, Minou. It took me three months before I dared taste it, but it's worth it. Eating it is like spinning fast, arms stretched out wide. It is so old it has started crying. Look,' he said, and held it up for me to see the small tears that covered it. 'Theodora liked cheeses too.' Priest blew his nose again.

'Did she like the smelly one?

'I am not sure, Minou. But she was a woman of great courage, and she never shied away from interesting experiences. And she did like the smell of many things: the salt, the bricks, her philosophy books and her goat. It's strange,' Priest continued, 'I have started to smell oranges everywhere. It's like your mama is baking again.' He sniffled and reached for his origami paper. 'She loved my oven. She always asked for my pretzel recipe. I kept saying no, but I am sorry now of course.' He looked at me apologetically.

'She is coming back, Priest,' I said matter of factly. 'But you can give the recipe to me if you want.'

I thought that being able to make pretzels might be useful. I could bake some for No Name and he could wear them around his neck. And if I got really good I could make them into hoops.

Priest looked uncertain. 'I will think about it, dear Minou, I will think about it.' He swiftly changed the subject. 'Did you know, Minou, that priests write to me from all over the world? They want this posting because of the oven.' Priest beamed. 'I didn't realise how many men of God there are who like baking. One day I will show you the photographs.'

'Of them?' I asked.

'No, no, Minou, of their cakes, of course,' said Priest, reaching for his handkerchief.

Once I told Priest that Mama's baking had failed yet again and that No Name was busy eating the left-overs of her orange cake. He left the church without a word, and strode towards our house, ending up in front of Mama's closed bedroom door. She was crying and wouldn't let him in, but Priest didn't seem to mind. 'Come and see me at church on Sunday,' he shouted happily. 'Bring your recipe book. Under God's roof, and with my industrial oven, nothing can go wrong. You have seen my pretzels.'

Mama kept sobbing, but Priest wasn't deterred. 'I am preparing a special sermon this week. Join us; the more the merrier.'

Priest had been preaching Genesis for a long

time. Some parts had even turned into song. It was nice to know the words, and No Name and I would sing along. But I thought it would be exciting if Priest talked about something else.

The following Sunday, however, the sermon was the same, and Mama arrived just as No Name and I were saying goodbye to Priest. She was wearing a bright pink apron and was carrying her black recipe book.

She embraced Priest with vigour and laughed. 'So this is where my rescuer lives.'

Priest blushed. 'Ah,' he said, 'God is the true rescuer. With a little help from my industrial oven, of course.'

I wasn't allowed to stay.

'I have to concentrate, Minou,' said Mama. 'I feel it might happen today.'

By late afternoon Papa started pacing the kitchen floor and No Name appeared on the door-step looking hopeful.

I was just about to boil water for coffee, when we heard Mama outside. We rushed to the door and there she was, singing with gusto, carrying a nice-looking cake decorated with a silver candle.

'Shoo,' she said to No Name when she passed him at the doorstep. 'Shoo, you silly dog.'

'What's the candle for?' I asked.

'To celebrate. Priest gave it to me, the dear man.' Mama laughed. 'I think it's the oven, but he is convinced that God has a part in it too. This one really did turn out right.'

Papa later told her how magnificent she had looked, walking towards the house, carrying the cake. 'You looked like a queen,' he declared, 'like Theodora.'

But Mama didn't like that. 'I look nothing like Theodora.'

'You looked stately,' Papa faltered, 'that's what I meant.'

'I was happy, that's all,' she said.

'You looked very, very happy, and beautiful too,' said Papa.

And Mama kissed him on the cheek.

I couldn't tell if the cake was any different from Mama's earlier efforts, but I ate slowly and tried to imagine what she might have felt, eating the same cake before the island, before she found Papa. And I wondered if there had been cakes in the war and whether her family had used an industrial oven just like Priest's.

* * *

Priest sneezed again, and his violet robes trembled. The church was getting colder and darker, and his nose was running.

'Are you sure you don't want a piece of cheese?' he asked.

I shook my head. The Old Cheese smelled terrible. 'How come you wanted to be a priest and not a baker?' I asked.

'I was longing.'

'What for?'

'God, Minou. We are all longing for God, even though we might think we long for something else.'

'Like what?'

'Oh, pretzels, or a horse.' He looked at me with a kind smile.

Logically I wasn't convinced. But it was hard to think philosophical thoughts while Priest's nose kept running.

The candles flickered and the cold crept through the picnic blanket. I wished I had put on an extra jumper.

'How do you keep warm at night?' I asked, thinking of priest's room upstairs next to the cold church bell, and his bed beneath the open window.

'With Theodora's bearskins, of course, but Minou,

you mustn't change the subject.' Priest blew his nose. 'We all long for God. But,' he reached for an origami sheet, 'it was easier when the Earth was flat.'

'What do you mean, Priest?'

'When it was flat you could only long for God in one direction. Now people look up and all they see is Galileo's stars. And when they look at the stars they forget about longing, and start counting constellations instead. They get confused.'

The talk of stars must have reminded Priest that it was night because he jumped to his feet with amazing speed.

'Minou,' he said, already out of breath as he ran towards the kitchen, 'could you climb upstairs and turn on the lights. And ring the bell. Just once, I think I need to hear it.'

I swiftly climbed the three flights of stairs and reached the small rectangular room. Moonlight fell across Priest's bed and the large copper bell. Above the bed was a framed photo. It showed Priest on a podium next to a short man with strong-looking arms, who I guessed might be Hoshami. They were both smiling at the camera. Next to the photo was a gold frame with a picture of Mother Mary, pretty in a blue dress, with a white dove in the palm of her hand.

I looked out through the window. The light from the moon illuminated the island and I could see our house with its snow-covered roof and the many ravens perched, black and motionless, along the rooftop. There was light in the kitchen and in Papa's study. I stretched over the windowsill and looked into Boxman's yard. No Name wasn't there. But Boxman was out shovelling snow in his cape. There was already a huge pile next to the open barn door. His shovel clunked, again and again, against snow and rocks.

And then I saw Mama.

Her long red hair, her pale face.

For a moment it seemed as if she looked my way.

'Mama,' I called out, 'Mama.' My voice echoed eerily in the bell.

But Mama didn't hear me. She turned and walked into Boxman's barn. I stood still and looked at the barn door for several minutes, straining, trying not to blink. But Mama didn't come back out.

I edged around the bell, and climbed down the stairs as quick as I could. Then I ran towards the entrance, past Priest and his picnic blankets.

'I have to go, Priest,' I called out, as I pulled at the large church door.

'But wait, Minou. Your notebook.' Priest joined me at the open door and handed me the book. 'Will you be all right walking home alone?'

On cue No Name appeared, wading through the snow towards us.

'Oh, you've got No Name. That's wonderful, Minou. Then goodnight, dear ones,' he said and closed the church door behind us.

I started to run. No Name tried to follow, but struggled in the snow, sinking deeper and deeper until he stopped with a howl. I turned around, picked him up, and ran on. I ran fast. Faster than the afternoon Papa had timed me. But this time Papa wasn't watching. No Name whimpered in my arms, and my stomach felt hot and my hair itchy. This wasn't how I had planned it. My jumper hadn't been washed for quite some time and I wished I was wearing a dress and had brushed my hair. But Papa didn't care much for clean clothes and neither did I. My story wasn't finished and my drawings were incomplete. And if Mama had already seen the dead boy, then she would have shown Boxman. And Boxman could make up stories much better than mine.

'Shh,' I said to No Name, trying not to slide in the snow. 'We are almost there.'

We heard the sound of Boxman's shovel before we reached the yard. No Name jumped out of my arms and staggered ahead of me towards the sound.

'Oh there he is,' Boxman called out when he saw us. 'I was about to go looking for him.' He picked up No Name and patted him.

I was inside the barn before Boxman had time to say anything else.

La Luna's blue box sat silently on the worktable. On a bale of hay stood a cup and saucer, half full of tea. Two of the apothecary's desk drawers, labelled 'Sugar', and 'Gifts for Unexpected Occasions', were open.

But the barn was empty. Mama wasn't there.

I lifted the lid of the finished box, but already knew that there would be nothing but air inside. I suddenly felt very tired.

'It's almost finished.' Boxman came up behind me.

'Why did you make her vanish?' I asked, but even as I said it, I knew she hadn't been there.

Boxman was quiet for a moment. 'Did you see your mama?'

I didn't answer.

He put an arm around me. 'It's because you miss her.'

I shrugged off his arm. 'Why do you have to make everything disappear?'

We all helped clean up at the end of the performance. The barn smelled deliciously of hay and candle wax. Boxman asked me to snuff the candles, while Priest collected pillows and Papa stacked the chairs.

'The pretzels are lovely, aren't they?' said Priest, crunching away, without noticing that no one else had touched them. 'I am very pleased with this batch.'

No Name was back in his cardigan, asleep. And neither Priest's unsuccessful attempts to feed him a pretzel, nor the two grey rabbits that hopped past, managed to wake him.

Boxman removed the spotlight from the ceiling, while Mama got changed behind the curtain. I was still wearing Bukowski's shoes and was getting good at walking in them.

After Papa finished stacking the chairs along the wall, he asked Priest, who was pacing near the door and peering anxiously into the rainy night, if he would like some company on the walk home. Priest looked gratefully at Papa, then thanked Boxman for a delightful evening.

Papa blew Mama a kiss, and said, 'Come home soon, I will make coffee for us.' Priest waved from the doorway, and we all shouted 'Goodbye, goodbye.'

'No,' I heard Papa say on the way out, 'I don't think she hurt herself. She has been practising. Yes. For many weeks.' And then from across the yard, 'The church does indeed look beautiful with all the light. Easy to find even in the rain.'

I finished snuffing the candles and Boxman climbed down from the ladder, took off his top hat and began to juggle the leftover pretzels.

'Have I ever told you,' he said to Mama, as one pretzel flew higher than the next, 'that few women act as well as you do in the box trick?'

Mama, who had been pushing hard on the suitcase in an attempt to lock it, smiled and leaned against the drawers. 'I knew that already,' she said, and caught one of Boxman's pretzels midair. Boxman juggled faster. Mama laughed and tried to catch another, but Boxman ducked and weaved. Mama laughed harder and pretzels flew higher each time. Then, without warning, she began to cry. She leant into Boxman, who let the pretzels fall to the floor and hugged her.

'Are you sad?' Boxman looked worried.

'Yes,' she said, and leant her head on his shoulder.

'Is it because of the vanishing act?' I asked.

'No, silly,' Mama tried to smile.

'You are a great performer,' said Boxman and gave her a squeeze. 'One of the best.'

I was waiting for Mama to say something that would explain her tears. But she wiped her eyes, laughed and said, 'No more of this nonsense.' She turned to me. 'Are you all right to walk back by yourself, Minou?'

'Yes, Mama.'

'I will be home soon. Then we will have coffee, the three of us. But first I need to help Boxman finish up.'

I was putting on my jacket when Boxman fetched his top hat from the apothecary's desk and ceremoniously placed it on my head. 'You were a great clown, Minou,' he said. 'This is for you. You deserve it.'

I went to the big mirror. The hat was large and fell onto my forehead. It had a big black velvet band and I thought it made me look mysterious, like a real magician.

'Your papa is waiting,' Mama prompted. 'Help him get the coffee ready.'

I blew them a kiss the way Papa had done and walked out into the rain. All the lights had been turned off and the yard was dark. The rain smelled of seaweed the way it often did before a storm, and I could hear a low rumble in the distance. Mama's laughter stopped and the whole island grew quiet.

The top hat was lovely and warm. I lifted my arms as Boxman did when he introduced Mama and made a circle in the air. I tried it again and whispered, 'Ladies and gentlemen,' then paused dramatically. 'You are about to see...of great renown...' I tried to say it the way Boxman did, making the word sound sweet; like one of the last apples in summer. I repeated, 'of great renown,' as I walked across the yard towards the forest path.

I was almost on the path when I heard something. It was a strange sound, a whimper almost. I stopped and listened. Then I heard it again. It sounded almost the way No Name did when he howled, but not as loud. I went back across the yard again, unsure. The barn door was ajar. Then I heard another whimper, soft and drawn out, and I leaned forward and looked through the crack. I couldn't really see anything, just the empty stage. The curtain hung heavily, drawn to the side. The mirror was leaning against the wall, and smoke from the snuffed candles was still hanging in the air. But then I saw a reflection in the mirror. At first I wasn't sure what it was. I reminded myself that Boxman could conjure up doves, rabbits, roses and coins and that nothing was unusual in his barn. But Mama's lips, her closed eyes, and Boxman's hand, his red-stone ring against her pale breast, looked real and not a trick.

Then I ran, my heart beating and fluttering like a leaf on a windy day. I was still wearing Bukowski's shoes and the path was slippery. And halfway through the forest I fell hard between two big pines. My chin and elbow hit the ground first. The top hat flew off and cold puddles of mud and water filled up the shoes and seeped through my clothes. But I didn't get up. I listened. The pine trees moved in the rain. Their grey reaching arms brushed against each other, again and again, like huge breaths, 'huu, huu huu'.

'Stop,' I shouted, furious at the pines. 'Stop moving, stop,' I shouted in a high-pitched howl. I got to my knees, close to crying. But I remembered Papa's words. I remembered that logic is a shield against snowstorms and years without apples on the apple tree. And I sat on the muddy path trying to remember Papa's favourite line from Descartes' *Meditations*, but it kept escaping me.

When I made it home Papa was standing in front of the stove, making pancakes, and I realised how cold I was.

'But, Minou, my girl' said Papa. 'What happened to you? You are covered in mud. And your face. Did you hurt yourself?'

The kitchen table was set with plates and cups. On each plate was a crane folded the way Priest had once taught Papa and me.

Papa helped me out of my wet clothes and put a blanket around me.

'What happened, Minou?' He attempted to brush the hair out of my face and I realised that I had forgotten the top hat in the forest. 'Have a pancake.' Papa handed me a large sugary pancake. 'We can start before your mama comes back. She won't mind. Is she still cleaning?'

I nodded, feeling shivery. I began to eat, and felt sorry for the serviette cranes. Their necks were too short.

'You didn't do their necks right.'

Papa followed my gaze and laughed. 'It wasn't as easy as I thought. Priest makes it look so simple. But

I wanted to do something special to celebrate. It was quite a performance tonight, wasn't it? How about your mama?'

I looked at Papa and felt again as if I was going to cry.

'The vanishing act, Minou.' Papa placed the jam next to me. 'She was phenomenal, wasn't she? And French, what a surprise. And I have never seen a better clown in my life.' Papa laughed. 'You scared Priest.'

I looked at Papa, feeling the pancake go cold in my hand.

'And No Name,' added Papa. 'The way he flew through those hoops. I must say, he is an interesting dog. So many talents. I wonder if Descartes liked dogs? I think the cardigan suited him.'

Papa poured coffee into the three cups he had lined up on the table. 'And what about the box trick, Minou? I know that there is logic behind it, but it looks real, doesn't it? Your mama is such a talented actress, I was about to run up and rescue her.'

'Papa,' I shook my head. 'Papa, I am not feeling well.'

But Papa didn't hear me. He was laughing. 'She would probably have liked that, don't you think, Minou?'

I stood up, unsure on my legs.

'Minou, what's the matter?'

'I want to go to the lighthouse, Papa.'

'But the coffee is ready. Don't you want to wait for your mama?'

I shook my head.

'How about you get washed and get into your own bed?'

'No, Papa.'

He put his hand on my forehead. 'I think you have a temperature, my girl. I don't know. Maybe we should wait for your mama to come back.'

'I want to go to the lighthouse, Papa. Now.'

'Well, then.' Papa looked hesitant. 'Do you want to take your coffee?'

I nodded, and put on the cardigan that Papa offered me. It was his, and far too big, but it smelled nicely of books and coffee.

'Descartes never said anything about magic. But then again, Minou, he died so young. Imagine all the things he would have said, if it hadn't been for that unfortunate time in Sweden.' Papa fetched my boots and wrapped a scarf around my neck. 'I am beginning to believe that magic is more enjoyable than I first thought.'

I left the kitchen unsteadily, and spilled most of the coffee as I climbed the stairs in the wind and rain. There was only a spoonful of brown sugar granules at the bottom of the cup when I put it next to the mattress and climbed under the blankets.

I woke in the lighthouse a few hours later. The storm had come and Priest was ringing the church bell again and again. Wind and rain moved forwards and backwards, as if clinging to each other in a never-ending wrestle. Papa was standing next to my mattress. He was bent over, a dark shadow next to the bulb, staring out the window in the direction of Boxman's barn.

'Papa.' I sat up, wide awake. 'What are you doing?'

'Sorry Minou,' he said, and started to retreat. 'I just wanted...your mama...I was trying to see if... go back to sleep, Minou...everything is fine.' And a rush of wind tore at my notebook as Papa opened the door to the staircase and left the lighthouse.

But I didn't go back to sleep. I dipped my finger in the coffee cup and scooped up the sugar as I peered through the foggy glass towards Boxman's barn. The rain obscured the view. I couldn't see the barn or even the forest path. All I could see in the bleak light from the downstairs windows was the edge of the forest where the wind pushed and pulled the trees. They looked like a dark sea.

Then Mama appeared. I wiped the glass. She stopped just out of the forest. Her dress hung wet and sagging around her. She stood holding her suitcase, framed by the moving pines, just looking at the house. I kept wiping the window, watching her, until she went inside.

Later I heard her shout. Her voice reached the lighthouse through the floorboards, like a wave crashing beneath Theodora's Plateau.

Boxman still had his arm around me. 'Your mama isn't here,' he said. He closed the lid of the blue box. 'She is dead, Minou. But I see her sometimes as well. When I least expect it. I miss her too.'

'I think you should give No Name a name,' I said. My voice sounded loud in the quiet barn. 'It's important to have a real name.'

'Then we need to think of a name, Minou.' He looked at me. 'Did you know that your mama used to see things too? She once saw a zebra standing where you are now. I knew straight away that it was Franz from my old circus. Franz wasn't very good at tricks and the circus wanted to send him to a slaughterhouse. I had to come up with something to save him.'

Boxman's voice started to sound like the wind far away over the ocean. But I nodded, feeling my head go heavy, as Boxman led me out of the barn.

'Come, Minou, let's get you home. Isn't it strange?' he said. 'I can smell your mama's orange cake. It makes me quite melancholy.'

Boxman kept talking about Franz as he steered me along the forest path. The stars were out, the moon climbed the trees and the snow squeaked beneath our feet.

'And then I remembered that Franz didn't like the accordion. Every time I played he would neigh in protest, but in a funny way it sounded as if he was singing. We ended up performing together until he died one summer morning, head resting on a tuft of grass in the paddock. He looked happy. It was a good way to die.'

Boxman had his arm around me as we walked. My eyes kept closing. For some reason I thought of Uncle and his investigation of the lighthouse, and how I had tried to draw a picture of him while he was searching for ghosts. Uncle was too tall to stand up in the tower, but I had given him a cushion to sit on. And, after admiring the big bulb, he folded his legs with slow, laboured movements, while I went and selected a red scarf out of my pile.

'What a view,' he said, as he wrapped the scarf around his neck with delight. 'Water everywhere, it feels like we are at the edge of the world.'

He switched on his ghost machine. Lights flashed and needles danced. He waved a microphone in different directions while turning one of the knobs up, then down.

I was trying to draw him looking scholarly and serious, but he kept moving around, and I couldn't get my drawing right. After a while I got my knitting out instead.

As Boxman guided me through the forest I remembered how relieved Uncle had looked when he turned off the machine. 'There is nothing to worry about, Minou,' he said. 'There are no ghosts here. The coast is clear...so to speak.'

'But lots of people went mad up here,' I protested, 'all the lighthouse keepers, because of the mercury.'

'That's unfortunate, Minou. But they are not here any longer. Most probably because of the ocean. Ghosts don't like water much.'

***

It seemed as if Boxman and I walked along the path forever. I drifted in and out of sleep and dreamed that I was caught in a howling snowstorm. Everything around me was white, and I shouted to No Name, who was wearing knitted gloves, 'Ahoy, ahoy, where is the edge of the world?'

No Name pointed into the distance and there was Franz, the zebra, singing, not realising how close he was to the surface of the deep, not knowing that he was about to fall in. I went to the edge and looked down, and saw Mama's hair, fanning out, pulling down, deeper and deeper. And from somewhere far away I heard Boxman's voice saying. 'I am sorry, Minou. I am so sorry.'

I woke in my bed downstairs. It was still night. My green jumper was tangled around me and my arm stuck in the sleeve. Papa must have helped me out of my boots and jacket, but I couldn't remember getting home or even saying goodbye to Boxman. And I couldn't remember going to bed.

I sat up. The ocean was grey with moonlight, and I could hear Boxman across the forest playing the accordion. I straightened my jumper, then got out of bed and walked across the corridor to the blue room. The colours on Mama's wall painting were muted in the moonlight, and a third raven had joined the other two in the windowsill. The dead boy looked calm beneath the frost, almost like he was sleeping.

'Sorry for disturbing you, dead boy,' I whispered as I closed the door again.

I found Papa working in the study, and saw straight away that Grandfather's postcards were no longer on the wall.

'My girl.' Papa turned towards me, his eyes looked sad, like the ocean before a big storm.

My hand felt for the postcard in my pocket. I had squashed it a bit in my sleep.

'Why did you take them down, Papa?'

Papa took off his fur hat and put it on the table. He rubbed his eyes. 'Your mama kept saying: "You can't reason about the war. It's not a reasonable thing. Search instead for what you love."' Papa picked up a pen from the table. 'I didn't understand it then. I just thought finding the truth might help. Your mama was so sad at times, and I keep dreaming about the cellar.'

'What was it like being in the cellar, Papa?'

Papa stared at the desk. I thought he hadn't heard me. But then he started to speak.

'Like I was forgotten. Alone in the whole world. There was no night, no day. Nothing. Just the smell of onions and carrots, and filth and soil. All I had was my mind. But even that turned against me.'

'How, Papa?'

'I kept thinking about milk. I didn't want to think of milk. If you think too much about something you haven't got, then it will break you. But I couldn't help it. In here'—Papa pointed to his forehead—'something reminded me of milk, always of milk.'

'But you don't like milk, Papa.'

'I do. Very much. But I don't drink it now because I cannot stand losing it again.'

Papa put on his reading glasses to inspect the book in front of him before putting it on the shelf. 'When the war finished it took them two months to find me. I couldn't straighten my legs and they had to carry me out. But the worst thing was that I didn't know if I wanted to come out. I no longer felt safe anywhere. I wanted to go back to the place where I had suffered so much. It didn't make any sense.

'When I came here, I had to learn everything all over. To walk, to see, to talk. It took me months before I could see colours again. Even the smallest bit of light hurt my eyes. But by the time your mama came I had my sight back, and what luck, because she was so beautiful, Minou. I have never met anyone as colourful as her.'

Papa straightened in the chair and rubbed his neck. Then he said, 'Boxman brought you home. We talked. About what happened.' Papa stared into the pretzels that swayed silently above us. 'I have shown him the dead boy, Minou. He is bringing a box tomorrow morning.'

I thought about Mama and how long it was since Boxman had come for morning coffee.

'Have some fish before you go to the lighthouse, my girl. I might sit with the dead boy for a little while, to say goodbye.' Papa turned to his desk again.

I didn't go to the lighthouse, instead I went back to bed. I lit a candle and sat facing the window with the blankets pulled over me. Boxman was still playing the accordion, and I heard Papa leave the study and open the door to the blue room.

I got the postcard from my pocket and read it again: '...it is in the heart and not in the words—not even in the most beautiful ones—but in the heart, in the skeleton bird pushing against your chest, wanting to fly, that we know for certain who and what we love. That is all we have, and all there is.'

I still didn't understand what it meant. But I thought of Papa in the cellar and how he didn't have any milk. And how his legs had been all bent. And

I thought about how Mama had said that Papa was asking the wrong question.

My notebook was next to me on the bed. Boxman must have carried it for me when he brought me home. I opened it.

I could hear Papa across the corridor, talking to the dead boy in the blue room. 'Dead boy,' I said aloud, hoping he might hear me, 'I will write you the end of the story.' And then I wrote. For a long time.

The sea was green and clear. Pirate was worried that there was going to be a storm. He looked into the water with a serious expression, while Monkey clung to his neck. 'It's not uncommon to get storms at the end of autumn,' he explained. But the boy wasn't scared. He thought Pirate could handle anything; he was after all a pirate.

The storm came later that day. Suddenly the air tasted awful, almost like sucking on a coin. Monkey hid in the box where the fishing nets were kept and then everything went black. There was no light, no horizon.

'This is just like being at home,' thought the boy, and he didn't enjoy it one bit. It started. The sea disappeared, and rose again like a wall around

them, over and over. Pirate shouted orders. The wood shuddered, the ropes stretched and they clung to whatever they could. They didn't know what was up or down, and it went on forever.

Then, with no warning, the blackness eased. It withdrew like a big sigh. The sea flattened, and dawn was painted on the horizon in two bold strokes. The boy started to cry in relief, but tried to hide it by helping Monkey out from the box. Just as they were about to go below deck, they realised that there must be an island close by. A tin of paint bobbed alongside the ship and it was then, when the boy stood leaning over the railing with a long hook, trying to fish the paint tin out, that she came floating by.

She was a foot beneath the water and she was beautiful, like a princess of the sea. Her arms were spread, her palms facing up and she was wearing a blue dress. Her skin was very white and her long red hair was moving like reeds. Fish swam around her, lots of fish, and she wore just one shoe. It looked as if the movements of the fish were carrying her forward. Pirate and Monkey came to the railing, and they all stood there looking at her until the boat sailed on.

The story made me sad. Terribly sad. My eyes started to hurt and my chest felt too big, as if no matter how much air I breathed in, it wasn't enough. Papa's mournful voice rose and fell from the blue room. And my lips started moving and I spoke too.

'You should not have left, Mama, you should not have taken Turtle. You should have stayed.'

Outside the window the moon shone on the snow cover. It stretched, sparkly grey, into the sea.

'Did you walk into the ocean, Mama? Or did the wind blow you over Theodora's Plateau?'

Papa's voice brushed against Boxman's accordion music, and against the sound of broken waves. I imagined Boxman in his cape, sitting on a bale of hay with the accordion. I thought of his red stone ring. And I thought of the circus and Mama in the darkened barn with him.

'Mama, you should have come home with me that night. Papa waited for you. For a long time. He wanted to tell you how good you were at singing.'

And they were my words, they came and they went and they travelled with Papa's, over the ocean, reaching the silverfin tuna, reaching the box at the bottom of the sea, reaching Galileo's stars and the end of the world. Then the words became sound and I heard Papa was crying too.

And across the forest No Name started howling, the accordion playing grew louder and it felt as if the whole island, the house, the tower, the ceiling was weeping. Then the church bell started, furiously, dong, dong, dong, dong, again and again.

In my belly was the froth of the sea, it kept welling up in my eyes, and I couldn't stop it. I choked and spat, and cried. And at last it all ended with a long lingering moan. After a while No Name stopped howling, the church went quiet, Boxman stopped playing and Papa fell silent.

Then I heard Mama's voice. 'You have grown, little one.'

I turned and looked out towards the sea and saw her sitting in a bathtub in the middle of the ocean. Her long hair was washed white in the moonlight. She gave me a wave and as I watched the bathtub move steadily through the water I imagined its clawed feet, cleaving through the sea.

I waved back, and then she was gone.

I woke in my bed the next morning to the drone of the delivery boat somewhere in the distance. I sat up slowly and looked out the window. The island was white and untouched.

I got out of bed and tiptoed to the blue room in bare feet. The three ravens were asleep, heads tucked under wings, and Papa slept in the armchair with the blanket wrapped around him. His fur hat had fallen off, but his ears looked warm despite the cold. I looked at the dead boy. More frost had covered his face and his bulked-up jacket with its shiny gold button. But he looked kind of happy beneath the frost. Maybe he had heard the drone of the delivery boat and was looking forward to being on a ship again.

I went straight to Mama's table and got the pale blue flower out of the old cookie tin.

'Papa,' I said, as I crossed the floor. But Papa didn't stir. I clipped the blue flower in my hair. 'Papa.' I shook his shoulder.

Papa opened his eyes, and shuddered.

'Is it morning?'

'Yes, Papa.'

'Is the boat on its way?'

'Yes,' I said.

'Then you better put some coffee on, my girl. Boxman and Priest will be here soon.' Papa rubbed his eyes, and looked at the dead boy. 'It's been quite something having him here, hasn't it, Minou?'

I nodded.

Then I went to the kitchen. I picked up my boots near the door and held on to Mama's shoe rack as I pulled them on. I looked at her shoes on the rack, then picked one up and held it against my cheek. It was dark brown suede and smelled of leather and the sea. At that moment I noticed that the kitchen felt good, like the time we had scrubbed the floors before Uncle visited. The orange smell had gone.

Just as the water was boiling Priest arrived carrying a small white cardboard box. He seemed cheerful with no signs of a cold.

'Have you seen the ravens on your rooftop, Minou? They have all left the church tower, I didn't know where they had gone. It's most peculiar.' He put the box on the table.

'What's in the box?' I asked.

'Wait and see,' said Priest and winked at me. 'Make me a coffee and I will show you.'

'You don't have a cold anymore,' I said, scooping coffee into the pot.

Priest wandered into the living room. 'I had the most extraordinary dream last night,' he called out to me. 'I dreamed your mama was in a boat right in the middle of the ocean, such a funny boat, almost like a bathtub. She waved to me and I felt so much better when I woke up.'

I could see Priest through the doorway, studying Mama's painting of The Great Shine and his tiger on the living room wall.

'Isn't that silly, Minou?' he said, sounding happy.

I got the sugar out of the cupboard, knowing that Priest liked four teaspoons in his coffee.

'I should have asked your mama,' he continued, 'to decorate the church while she was still with us. She could have painted the rabbits and No Name and all the things on the island. Theodora would have enjoyed that.'

'Mama would have liked that too,' I said.

Priest nodded. 'Do you mind if I have a look in the blue room, Minou?' He moved towards the corridor. 'It's so long since I last admired the painting of her arrival.'

But before Priest reached the door to the blue room I remembered that he knew nothing about the dead boy. 'The box you brought, Priest,' I called out, 'it's moving.'

It was true. The box had skidded to the edge

of the table. It was about to fall when Priest rushed back and grabbed it.

At that moment No Name barked and Boxman's wheelbarrow clunked against the house.

No Name was wearing his scarf and ran in ahead of Boxman, who stamped his boots free of snow on the mat. He noticed the box straight away. 'Are you doing a magic trick?' he asked Priest.

'No, no,' said Priest. 'It's for Minou. It's a gift.'

'Cardboard boxes are good for magic, I can teach you some tricks.'

Priest was gracious. 'I only use boxes for gifts, dear Boxman,' he answered. 'Magic scares me a little.'

'That reminds me.' Boxman swung his cape open and withdrew a small pineapple from the inside pocket. 'This is for you, Minou. It will cheer you up. Pineapples are funny. You looked so small and tired yesterday.' He stopped. 'But, Minou. You are wearing a flower in your hair. You look beautiful.'

'I thought there was something different about you, Minou,' said Priest. 'I must say, that pale blue suits you. It's almost the same colour as Mother Mary's dress. The one she wears in my picture.'

The coffee had just started boiling when Papa

came out of the blue room. He looked the way he did once when dancing with Mama in the kitchen, slowly, round and round, his hand resting on her back, as though he knew every step they were meant to take. And Mama was quiet. She didn't laugh or talk or get angry; she gazed at him with eyes like a quiet sea.

'You can open the box now, Minou,' said Priest. 'I was waiting for your papa.'

Everyone gathered around the table as I lifted the lid. And there, beneath five layers of tissue paper, sat Turtle, the morning light reflected in his blind eyes. He blinked, and No Name barked.

'Cheers to Turtle,' shouted Priest, startling us all. Then he laughed boisterously. 'He is alive, Minou, he is alive. I didn't understand where all my pretzels were going. But look, he has grown fat. He was behind the cross all this time, I think he might have found God. He looks a lot happier.'

And Turtle definitely looked both happy and chubby as he stared blindly at all of us.

'Maybe he should live inside from now on,' said Papa, who was pouring coffee for everyone. 'It might be too cold for him to go under the steps again, especially if he has been near an oven all this time.'

'An industrial oven,' added Priest.

I looked at Turtle and remembered the sound of rain and Mama's shoes across the floor, and the moment when she paused to open the black umbrella and pick him up.

The boat horn sounded again, this time closer, and Papa put down his cup.

'Priest,' he said, 'don't be alarmed. There is something you need to see.'

'Alarmed, but why?' Priest placed the lid back on the box.

'Follow me.'

I carefully put Turtle on the floor. Then I ran after them and reached for Priest's hand just as he entered the blue room. But Priest didn't get scared. He studied the boy calmly, and Papa explained everything, starting from the moment I had found him on the beach, dusted with new snow in a cradle of rocks.

Priest moved closer. 'He looks kind,' he said. 'As if you could confess all your sorrows to him.'

Papa agreed. 'We will be sad to see him leave.

The box for the dead boy had J.G. Magician written on the side.

'It's a spare,' Boxman explained with laboured breath, as he and Papa tried to lift the dead boy from the bed into the box. 'J.G. died before it was finished and his wife didn't want it. She didn't want to pay for it either.' The boy didn't move and Papa and Boxman tried to lift him again. Boxman continued, 'She sent me a letter saying, "I despise magic and do not require the box."'

'You are going back on a ship,' I said, trying to encourage the dead boy, because suddenly it looked as if he didn't want to go, as if he was trying his hardest to stay on the bed.

'Imagine, a dead boy on this island,' said Priest, standing aside for Papa who went around the bed to get a better grip.

'He is too heavy,' said Papa. 'You have to help Boxman with the legs, Minou.'

'If only I had time to prepare a sermon for him,' said Priest, looking regretful.

I took hold of his feet. 'He is very cold, Papa.'

'Yes, my girl.' Papa was puffing. 'Yes he is. Let's lift on three.'

The dead boy didn't fit into the box. His bent leg sat stiffly above its edge, as Papa had predicted. Boxman went to fetch some rope to secure the lid, and I ran to the lighthouse to get the orange scarf.

Priest wanted to say a prayer for the dead boy. And when Boxman came back we all gathered around the box. No Name tried to jump in with the dead boy, but Priest grabbed him by the scarf and dragged him back. The three ravens observed the commotion silently from the windowsill.

The dead boy's face was pale. Most of the frost had melted during all the activity, and I thought that he looked nice in his red sock and orange scarf. Priest cleared his throat and spoke with a calm voice, 'May the sun shine upon you. May you feel God in the salt and the sea. And may you see Jesus' feet beneath his robe, and remember that, even though he was the son of God, he too was a humble traveller.'

And I thought about Mama in the sea, floating like a sea princess. And I thought that somehow Priest's prayer was for her as well.

'We might just have time to finish our coffee before we secure the lid,' said Papa. And then he left the room with Priest and Boxman.

No Name and I stayed with the dead boy, listening to Priest's joyous laughter from the kitchen and the clinks of coffee cups. But when No Name tried to jump into the box once more, I pushed him out of the room and closed the door in his desperate face.

I put the postcard back in the bottle and returned the shoe to the box. No Name whimpered outside the door. 'Go away, No Name,' I whispered. Then I tore out my story from the notebook. 'This is for you, dead boy,' I said, as I lifted his frozen jacket and placed the pages in his pocket.

It still felt like he wanted something from me. I sat back for a moment and looked at him. And then I bent close and whispered my secret into his blue ear.

We placed the box on the wheelbarrow and pushed it out of the house, past the golden bowl and down the path. Priest ran alongside, holding up his robe, shouting, 'Careful, careful,' while the wheelbarrow bumped and jumped over rocks and ice, and No Name darted back and forth, barking.

Papa opened Theodora's gates, just as the boatmen lowered their dinghy into the sea. And then, in one go, the ravens left the roof, spreading like a black cloud over the forest, to Boxman's barn, to the church tower and a few flew boldly out beyond the reef to meet the boatmen.

'I have missed them in the tower, I hope they all come back,' said Priest. 'They make such comforting noises in the night.'

And as we were waiting on the beach, hearing the boatmen swearing out beyond the reef, Papa bent to pat No Name. Priest started telling Boxman that Theodora had made plans to build a theatre on the island just before she died, with curtains and a wooden stage, varnished so no one would get hurt if they had bare feet.

Then I felt it. I felt the skeleton bird in my chest, pushing its wings against my ribs, wild and hard, as if it was about to fly, as if it was about to take off, and I knew with absolute certainty, clearly and distinctly, that I loved them all. It was all I had and all there was. I turned and looked at the snow-covered island. One day I was going to pack Mama's red suitcase full of things and take Turtle. One day I was going with the boatmen to see China, the way Mama had wanted to do. When I was ready, but not yet.

I faced the sea again. The boatmen were coming closer. A raven swooped out of the sky and dived in a glorious arc towards the waves.

'Here they come,' said Papa.

ACKNOWLEDGMENTS

My heartfelt thanks to Michael Heyward and Caro Cooper of Text Publishing, Dr Anne Brewster, Dr Shalmalee Palekar and Dr Andy Kissane of University of New South Wales, as well as Narelle Jones and Angela O'Keeffe. You were all instrumental in bringing this book to life.

And to Matilde Martin, Andrew Shine, Deb Saffir, Vicki Hansen, Emily Sarkadi, Digby Clarke, Ester Sarkadi-Clarke, Trish Tagg, Nicky Esplin, Chris Lambert and Simone Fraser, thank you so much for your encouragement and feedback during the writing process.